ONE NIGHT

WILL ONE NIGHT BE ENOUGH?

NICOLA C. PRIEST

OTHER BOOKS BY NICOLA C. PRIEST

One Night

Copyright © Nicola C. Priest 2020

Cover Illustration by Francessca Wingfield
Cover Photography by James Critchley

Editor: Stephanie Farrant at Farrant Editing

ACKNOWLEDGMENTS

Here I am again, book number eight, and I still struggle to write these. So this time, I'm thanking people who have had a hand, either directly or indirectly, in getting this book ready for publication.

This book wasn't on my radar until I saw, and fell in love with, the cover. I even kept the title she used when creating it. I'm sure you'll all agree that it is eye catching and beautiful, and for that, I need to thank four people:

Francessca Wingfield, for her epic design skills in creating the cover.
James Critchley, for his wonderful photographic talents in capturing the image.
&
Megan Jessica Taylor and Zac Smith, for your professionalism and on-camera chemistry, which helped to create such a stunning image.

Once I've written the book, another lady then gets involved to give the words a polish and get the story ready to send out to the masses:

Stephanie Farrant, your editing style is exactly what I need to make my books the best they can be. You're my go-to girl for constructive criticism, and you're not afraid to tell me when something isn't working. I love you for that, so thank you.

Most of this book was written while I was starting out in a new job, with a new team, and new people. Thankfully, everyone welcomed me with open arms and made me feel like I was part of the team from day one. It made everything easier for me, so the only thing I had to worry about was getting this book written. Thank you, Andy, Jane, Tracey, Jackie and Robin.

Last but by no means least, the readers. I can't thank you enough for your continued support. If it weren't for you taking a chance on me and spending your hard-earned money buying my books, I wouldn't be doing this. I will be eternally grateful.

1

_____

"*C*ongratulations again, Miss Fox. We look forward to welcoming you to Creativity in Design in two weeks' time."

"Thank you, Mr Brendan. I look forward to seeing you then."

I end the call and just stare at the phone in my hand. After a moment, I toss it onto my bed, before I start jumping up and down and pumping my fists.

I've done it. I've only bloody gone and got my dream job. Well, maybe not my ultimate dream job, but it is definitely a step in the right direction. To say I am surprised is an understatement. I only recently completed my design qualifications, so when I saw the job advertised online, I applied for it just for the hell of it.

I planned on using the interview process as practice, until I had the chance to get some experience under my belt. Then I figured I could really go for it, give my all in any interviews and actually sound like I know what I'm talking about, rather than making a fool of myself. Never in my wildest dreams did I think I would actually be successful, certainly not on the first attempt.

Oh, in case you were wondering why I'm dancing around my room like a mad woman, it's because I just received the call offering me the job as executive assistant to one of the interior designers at Creativity in Design. The job includes full training, so one day, I can move up the ranks and become a designer myself. I can't believe I got so lucky.

"Eleanor, will you stop jumping around up there. You're going to come through the ceiling."

"Sorry, Mum."

I look towards the bedroom door and childishly stick my tongue out. There's one other good thing about this new job: it's over two hundred miles away, in Porthcurno, on the south coast of England. No more parents watching my every move. I can finally be my own woman, no longer having to explain where I'm going or when I will be back, and don't even get me started on my brother.

He is six years older than I am and takes his role as big brother to the extreme. If any guy dares to even look at me, he gives them a stare that could stop traffic. I was *seventeen* when I got my first real boyfriend, and that lasted about five minutes as he couldn't cope with the 'big brother' scrutiny. When I got together with Stuart, my current boyfriend, I had to have words with Eric, telling him to lay off his usual crap, which he did for the most part. Which reminds me, I need to call Stuart to tell him the good news.

I grab my phone from the bed and find his name in the contacts, hesitating as I go to press the call button. No, I'm not going to call him. I'm going to go around to his place and tell him the news in person. I want him to see how happy I am that I've been given this opportunity.

He hadn't been too keen on me applying for the position,

mainly because of how far away it was, but I'm pretty sure I talked him around, convincing him that after four years together, we could make a long-distance relationship work. I hope that when I tell him I got the job, and he sees how much it means to me, he will be the supportive boyfriend he keeps telling me he wants to be.

I grab my bag and drop in my phone. After fishing out my car keys, I bolt from my room and down the stairs, stopping short when my mum comes out of nowhere to stand in front of me, blocking my path.

Formidable isn't usually a word used to describe women, but it fits my mum perfectly. She likes things done a certain way, and if anything, or anyone, deviates from that, God help you. She has her daily routine planned to within minutes, and if I had to guess, I'd say she hadn't planned on me going out right now, which explains the almost pissed expression on her face.

She's looking at me over her glasses, which she has perched on the end of her nose. She reminds me of one of those school mistresses who is about to tell off an errant child who won't behave in class.

"Where are you going? Dinner is almost ready."

"I'm going round to see Stuart."

"I've cooked for three people, Eleanor. Did it not occur to you to let me know sooner?"

"It's not like that, Mum. I've just received some good news I want to share with him. If I'd known about it earlier, I would have told you. I won't be too long."

"Well if you're not back in half an hour, you can sort out your own dinner. Your father and I are not going to wait around for you."

With that, my mother walks into the kitchen, and I just sigh while shaking my head. I shouldn't be surprised that my mum didn't ask what my good news is. I can't remember a time when my parents actually took an interest in what I do, unless it affects them in some way. Sometimes, I wonder why they even had children in the first place. No, scratch that, why they hadn't stopped when they had my brother.

The man can do no wrong in their eyes. To them, he is the perfect son, and he does all he can to live up to their ideal image, even though I know it pisses him off at times and forces him to be someone he isn't. *Sometimes, Ellie, it's just easier to be what they want than it is to try and be myself.* The fact that he truly believes that saddens me.

Eric is working in a job he hates, just to keep them happy. He is in a relationship with a woman he doesn't love, and I know he wants nothing more than to move further away from them. At the moment, he lives on the same street, five doors away, just so he can be there when our parents need him to do something they feel is beneath them. Oh, they'd never say that, but it's clear to anyone who knows them that they think they're better than most.

I wish Eric would just tell them where to go, but he won't because he knows as soon as he does, they will lay a guilt trip on him so thick he will probably end up moving back in with them just to shut them up.

Don't get me wrong, I love my brother to bits, but sometimes I get so frustrated with his unwillingness to stand up for himself, even if it does upset our parents. Sometimes I just want to throttle him. Too many times I have watched him do something for them that he doesn't want to do, like cancel plans so he can be at their beck and call. It hurts me to watch it happen, but I know that no matter what I say to him, only he can change it.

I will always be there for Eric if he needs me, but I will now do it from the coast. As for my parents, well, I love my parents, but they seem to forget that I'm not a little girl anymore. Hell, they sometimes forget they even have a daughter. I doubt they'll even notice I'm gone, until they need something, that is. I'm a twenty-one-year-old woman with my own mind and my own life, and I am going to show them I can stand on my own two feet.

I secure my bag on my shoulder as I leave the house and jump in my car. It's only a short drive to Stuart's house, and I can't wait to get there to share the good news. He'll be happy for me; I'm sure of it.

Less than five minutes later, I'm stopping my car outside the house Stuart shares with his cousins, Joe and Mitch. I know they are away on their annual family holiday, so Stuart will be home alone tonight. Climbing out of the car, I lock it, and then find the key to his front door on my keychain as I walk up the drive.

Within seconds I'm pushing the key into the lock and entering the house. It's eerily quiet, and I check my watch, seeing it's just before 6pm. I expected Stuart to be back from work by now, but there is no sign of him. I drop my bag on a nearby chair and sit on the sofa, preparing to wait for him to return, when I hear a thud from upstairs.

So, Stuart is home after all. Smiling, I stand and make my way upstairs. When I reach the landing, the door is slightly ajar, and I can hear music playing, so I move forward and rest my hand against the wood before pushing the door open.

I take one step into the room before freezing, taking in the sight of my boyfriend's naked backside as he bends over the bed, his lips attached to the obviously fake breast of a brunette.

A brunette that isn't me.

I'm rooted to the spot. My heart is racing, and my vision blurs as my hands close into fists at my sides. My chest hurts, and I refuse to acknowledge that my heart could possibly be breaking. My head is telling me to scream and shout at him; to lay into him with all the strength I have. I want to reach out and drag him off her, then slap him right across that too hand-some face for cheating on me, but I don't.

I give them one last look, before taking a deep breath. I turn and exit the room before making my way back down-stairs, grabbing my bag, and leaving the house, making sure to slam the door as loudly as I can on my way out. When I'm back in my car, I feel the tears building behind my eyes. I have so many friends who've had trouble with men; friends who have cried rivers because of men. I'm not going to give him the satisfaction of doing the same.

No man is worthy of my tears; even one I thought I might spend the rest of my life with. If he thinks so little of me that he can cheat on me after two years together, and in the very same bed I slept in only two nights ago, then he can go to hell. He doesn't deserve me, and I am better off without him. Sure, my heart hurts with the knowledge that what we had is now over, but I will move on from it.

Eventually.

Straightening my back and squaring my shoulders, I start the engine and take one more look at the house, seeing a topless Stuart peering down from the bedroom window. After putting the car in gear, I start to pull away, but then I hit the brake, just long enough to flip my middle finger at the man I hope I never see again.

2

~ Two weeks later ~

"*Y*ou know, Ellie, this could be the last time we get to go out together for a while, seeing as you are swanning off to the coast for God knows how long."

I roll my eyes at my friend as she switches off her straightening iron. Becky has been spouting the same nonsense all week, ever since I called her to say I wanted one night out, so I can just let loose and not worry about anything before I move away for my new job.

For some reason, Becky is convinced we won't see each other again, and she isn't letting me forget it. Becky has been my friend for close to fifteen years, and I know she knows it will take more than two hundred miles to dent that friendship. Even knowing that information, she is still doing her damndest to make me feel guilty about going.

Not that I expected anything different. Becky is a great friend, and I wouldn't change her for anything, but she does have a tendency to be a little selfish at times. Not to mention she hates change. When Becky is comfortable with something, she is the nicest person you could ever wish to meet, but when things change, even slightly, she can't handle it, and she goes into 'how will it affect me' mode.

So, when I announced that I got the job and would be moving away for said job, Becky had gone straight into her default mode rather than congratulating me and asking how I felt about it. I know she is happy for me in her own way, but she has difficulty showing it.

"Will you quit it, Becky? You're talking as if I'm moving to the other side of the world. It's a four-hour drive. My new place has a spare bedroom, so you can visit whenever you want. It's not like we're never going to see each other again."

I glance at her in the mirror as she starts to apply her makeup. She doesn't need it. Becky is one of those girls who would be called a natural beauty and uses makeup to enhance what she already has; smoky grey eyes, full pouty lips, and skin as soft as a baby's backside, to use the common phrase. She's a natural blond too, which can't be said for many of my friends, and I swear no one believes her, when she says it doesn't come from a bottle.

I love her to bits, but sometimes even I get jealous of how she looks. I mean, when you have friends, you like to think of yourself as the pretty one. I do anyway, even if I know deep down that's not really the case, not with a girl who looks like Becky as my friend.

When Becky looks away, I swear I see her pouting at me, and I just roll my eyes again as I continue to apply shadow to my eyelids. I let my mind wander to everything that has happened over the last two weeks.

Since I found out about the job, I've been so busy arranging everything that I haven't really had a chance to stop and think about anything else. I've been really lucky with the place I've found to live when I'm down there. I've always been dubious when I heard people say they found something through 'a friend of a friend,', but that's exactly what happened with me.

I'd gone for my monthly manicure, when I started talking about the new job. I mentioned that I wasn't having any luck finding a place to stay, as everywhere was either too expensive or too far out of town, and the manicurist had given me the phone number for her aunt and uncle. She explained they had a place they were looking to rent out, as they were moving to Canada.

I called them that afternoon, and after they sent me some photos of the house, I fell in love with the place almost immediately. As they had no mortgage, they didn't want a fortune in rent, so after a little negotiating, I signed a six-month rental agreement with the option to extend, depending on how the job goes.

The house is gorgeous and has spectacular views over the town and beach at Porthcurno. There are two double bedrooms, one of which an en-suite, and a large family bathroom. The living area is pretty much open plan and includes a large archway that leads into the kitchen and dining room.

From the pictures I've seen, the whole cottage has been decorated in neutral or pastel colours, which I prefer, but the owners told me if I plan on staying there long-term, I can decorate however I want.

The outside of the property is just as beautiful as the inside. It has a wraparound porch that goes along the front and one side of the cottage that has room for a small table and a couple of chairs. There is also a porch swing that I've been told has only been there a few weeks and has never been used. I'll be able to see the beach from the porch, and a fifteen-minute walk will take me down to the sand and the sea.

There is a small garden at the back, which, luckily, isn't overlooked by any of the neighbouring properties, so maintaining my privacy won't be an issue.

The couple bought the little cottage with the intention of making it a holiday rental, but found they loved the area so much they decided to make it their main home.

When their only daughter moved to Canada with her husband, they visited whenever they could. Now that their daughter has given birth to their first grandchild, they have decided to move to Canada permanently. They hadn't wanted to sell the property, as they loved it so much, so when they heard I needed a place to stay, well, the rest, as they say, is history.

Today is Friday, which means I have what is left of today and tomorrow before I have to start packing up my car with what little I have and begin the four-hour drive down to Porthcurno. I start my new job on Monday, and I can't bloody wait.

I've spoken with my new boss several times over the last week, a lady called Isobel Langley. She is only a few years older than me, and like me, she started out as an executive assistant. Just speaking with her and listening to her stories has made me feel more confident that I will be able to do this job. It has also given me more confidence concerning the company's pledge to put me through the training I need.

I have to admit, I was a little dubious when they told me about the training opportunities. I mean, what company pays for someone to get qualifications to do a job, when they could just hire someone who already has them? My friends all thought the same, but now that I have spoken with someone who has gone through it, I'm more positive about taking the position.

Isobel has told me that for the first few days, I will just be shadowing her and learning more about the company. I've done some research of my own, so I know the company has been around for just over ten years and was built from the ground up by two brothers, Kyle and Kevin Brendan.

The biography on the brothers says they had only been nineteen and twenty-two when they started the company, after inheriting money from their late grandfather. They both still appear to be very hands on with the business, one managing the money side of things, the other being the creative arm in the partnership. Isobel spoke very highly of the brothers, and I'm excited to meet them, not to mention to thank them for giving me the opportunity they have.

After fifteen minutes, Becky and I are both ready to go. We've both gone for a little black dress, with Becky opting for blood red heels with matching clutch, where I've gone for silver accessories. Our taxi is on its way, and as we start down the stairs, we ignore the disapproving looks being thrown at us by my mother. Within seconds, we are in the confines of the car, discussing where we're going to end up later tonight.

I've told Becky that I want a night out with no holds barred. I've been so well behaved for the last two years, mainly due to being with Stuart, but now he is out of the picture, I want to let loose. I want to get drunk; I want to dance until my feet beg me to stop; and most of all, I want to laugh, shout, and have a whole lot of fun.

Yes, tonight is going to be one of those nights I want to both remember and forget.

3

"*W*oohoo! I have never felt so alive," I scream at the top of my voice, so Becky can hear me over the music.

Somehow, and I have no idea how, we have wound up in a nightclub in the middle of town. Despite my initial desire for an 'anything goes' night, we decided at around midnight that we would stick to the cocktail bars. Now it's almost 3am, and we've been dancing non-stop for the last hour.

We have worked our way down several cocktail menus, and I have no idea what the bluey-green concoction is that I'm holding in my hand, but it tastes delicious.

"Me too," Becky shouts back, before giving me a nudge. "I think you've pulled, Ellie."

I down the rest of my drink then put the glass on a nearby table as I turn to Becky, whose gaze has settled on something over my shoulder. I look in the same direction. My eyes connect with a pair of green orbs, and I experience what feels like a bolt of electricity shoot through me. His look is so intense, my whole body heats up from the core.

"He's been watching you for the last twenty minutes."

I hear her voice close to my ear but pay it no mind. The guy across the room has my full attention, and I'm not sure why he is drawing me in so strongly and so easily. I don't even have a clear view of what he looks like; all I can see are those eyes, and they are enough for me to know he can cause me a whole lot of trouble.

"You said you wanted to have fun tonight. Why not go and have some fun with that guy? You're practically naked in his eyes anyway, and, by the way, you're staring back. I'd say he is at least topless in yours."

Becky's right. I did come out tonight for one last blow out before moving away. A one-night stand hadn't been part of my plan, but why the hell not? We're both adults, and as long as he is willing, what's the harm?

After receiving a little nudge from Becky, I start to move forward, and before I know it, I'm standing in front of the guy with the bright green eyes that tracked me across the room. Now that I'm in front of him, I can see him more clearly.

Even in my heels I only come up to his chest. He is easily a few inches above six feet, and I'm not sure if it's because of the alcohol swimming in my veins, but he looks as wide as he is tall. His biceps are straining the material of the white shirt he's wearing, with the sleeves rolled up to his elbows, and I can see a series of intricate tattoos running down his left arm to his wrist.

I lift my eyes back to his face, seeing a square jawline covered with light stubble. His hair looks to be a dirty blond and is shorter at the sides than on top. I decide right there and then that if this guy is amenable to the idea, a one-night stand won't be a completely bad idea.

"My friend says you've been watching me," I say as he leans down to hear me.

"I have," he replies, his deep voice easily heard over the music.

"Why?"

"Honestly?" When I nod, he leans in closer, his hand going to my waist, his breath fanning across my neck. "Because I want to see what you're hiding under that little dress you have on, and then I want to fuck you hard against a wall until you scream."

I feel my pulse spike, and my body begins to tremble. No guy has ever spoken to me like that before, never mind a man I have literally just met. When he takes my hand and places it over the front of his trousers, my eyes go wide. He is rock hard behind the material, and when my fingers instinctively flex around him, I see his eyes darken.

He is big. No, he is huge, easily bigger than anyone I've been with in the past. I can feel the heat between my legs, and when I move my hand slightly, I'm sure I hear him growl, the deep sound making my decision easy.

Taking a step closer, so I'm almost pressed against him, I lift my eyes to his, angle my head so I can speak in his ear, and say, "Where do you want to take me?"

Leaning away from him, I see him grin down at me before he grabs my hand and leads me through the crowd. I struggle to keep up with him in my heels, but within seconds, he's pulled me into a room, closed the door, and his mouth is on mine.

I have mere seconds to adjust to what is happening, but when I feel his hands begin to tug at the neckline of my dress, I let myself go. I kiss him back as if my life depends on it, my fingers working the buttons on his shirt until I feel the fabric part.

When my back hits the wall, he breaks the kiss, and I glance down to see what the opening of his shirt has revealed.

My mouth begins to water as I take in a firm chest peppered with tattoos, and abs that cause me to want to lick along every defined muscle. When he kisses me again, his tongue pushes past my lips. I allow him entry as my hands trail over the firm skin of his torso, before moving up to grip his hair tightly.

I can't believe I'm doing this. There's a little voice inside my head that is calling me all sorts of names, but I ignore it as waves of pleasure wash through me. His hands run up and down my body, lifting the hem of my dress until it's around my waist.

His lips release mine and move down to my now exposed breasts. I let my head fall back against the wall as he takes my nipple between his teeth and tugs gently. I can't stop the moan that passes my lips as a bolt of pure pleasure shoots through me.

"I knew you'd be like this. I want to fuck you so badly."

His words are doing wondrous things to my insides, and as if giving permission, I lift my leg and wrap it around his back, silently thanking God when he catches me as I jump. I'm now pinned against the wall by his chest and his hips. He releases me momentarily, and with a bit of creative manoeuvring, he manages to sheath himself with a condom before pulling my knickers aside and plunging deep inside me.

I cry out at the intrusion, feeling my body stretching to take him. There is a sharp burst of pain at the initial entry, but when he begins moving, pleasure quickly becomes the overriding sensation as I grip his shoulders and let him move inside me.

"Fuck you're tight," he says as he struggles to catch his breath. "I need to fuck you hard."

All I can do is nod, as my ability to form a coherent sentence appears to have vanished, along with my inhibitions, somewhere between entering the room and him putting his lips on me. When he puts his hands under my thighs and presses me more firmly against the wall, I cling to his shoulders as he begins pounding into me.

The grunts and groans coming from him only make me want him to go faster, and I try to move against him, but he is holding me so tightly that all I can do is hold on and hope I come out the other side in one piece.

I can feel the tell-tale tightening in my stomach before it spreads through my limbs as everything in me begins to tremble. I am so close to what I know will be the strongest orgasm I've experienced as he continues to hammer into me. My hands are on his shoulders, then his arms, then in his hair, before I move them down to my breasts and squeeze, seeing his eyes darken at my actions.

"Fuck yes," he groans when I close my eyes and arch my back as the first wave of pleasure begins to wash over me, my legs locking tightly around his waist, pulling him deeper inside me.

After three more punishing thrusts, he roars as his release rips through him, and his head falls forward onto my shoulder. Both of us are breathing quick, ragged breaths, and I wince when he pulls out of me a few minutes later.

I slowly let my legs fall from his hips and my feet connect with the floor. We both stay where we are for several minutes until our breathing returns to normal. I'm pleased he's still holding me, as I'm not quite sure I've regained the strength in my legs just yet. When he lifts his head and straightens, I realise he is taller than I first thought, though it probably has something to do with the fact I am now barefoot, my shoes having fallen off with the force of his thrusts.

"You okay?"

Still unable to speak, I just nod and give him a small

smile as he reaches out and fixes my dress until I'm covered again, before he adjusts himself and zips his jeans.

"Do you need a minute?"

"Yeah," I reply, suddenly feeling a little self-conscious and a whole lot slutty for what I'd just let happen.

"Okay," he says as he leans in, kissing my cheek, before vanishing from the room.

What the hell have I just done? I know I asked for a no holds barred night out, but that hadn't included a quickie in what I now see is an office, with a complete stranger, whose name I don't even know. Granted, it was one hell of a quickie, which resulted in probably the best orgasm I've ever had in my life, but I don't do that kind of thing.

As I lean against the door, I look around the room, seeing a mirror on the far wall. I cross over and peer at my reflection. From the neck down, I look pretty normal, but there is no way my face and hair can hide what went on only a few minutes ago. I've heard women refer to the 'just fucked look' and always wondered what it looks like.

Now I know.

My lips are red and swollen from our kisses, and my lipstick is smeared across my face. My hair is no longer sleek and straight but now slick with sweat and hanging in limp strands around my shoulders. I hastily run my fingers through my hair in an attempt to make it look half decent. Wondering how to sort my lipstick, I grab a tissue from a box on the desk and scrub my lips to get rid of the remaining colour.

There is very little I can do about the swollen lips and the glow on my cheeks. I just have to hope the dim lights out in the main club will hide them from view.

I turn around, find my shoes, and slip them back on my feet. Putting my hand on the door handle, I take a deep breath before opening the door and leaving the office.

My eyes are assaulted by the bright lights, which are in stark contrast to the dimness of the room I've just vacated. I head in the direction of where I left Becky, catching the eye of my one-night stand as I cross the room, seeing him smile and nod at me. I look away and see Becky dancing with a guy she was chatting to earlier in the night. I walk over to them and tap Becky on the shoulder.

"You ready to go, Becky? I think I've had enough for tonight."

I see the knowing smile Becky gives me as she untangles herself from the guy she is dancing with. I take her hand, and as we leave the club, I'm sure I can feel a pair of green eyes burning into my back.

4

———

$\mathscr{I}$t's a glorious Sunday afternoon, and I'm halfway through a four-hour drive to Porthcurno. The sun is shining, and I have my favourite music blaring. My car is loaded with suitcases and cardboard boxes that contain all the personal belongings that matter to me. When I eventually arrive, I will be spending the afternoon unpacking and getting my new home just as I want it before I start my new job in the morning.

Seeing a sign for the services, I indicate I'm leaving the motorway and pull in, knowing I won't be able to go another two hours without a toilet break. After finding a parking space, I turn off the engine and grab my bag before exiting the car. I wince slightly at the soreness between my legs; a soreness that reminds me of the most thrilling and embarrassing night of my life.

I still can't believe what I did that night, and Becky won't let me forget it either. On the ride home, Becky pestered me until I told her what had happened, and once I did, I didn't wait for her response. I dived out of the taxi and have avoided Becky's calls and texts since.

I know it's childish and a little ridiculous to avoid my best friend. Becky won't judge me, mainly because she's had her fair share of one-night stands herself, but I can't deal with her right now. I still feel stupid for letting myself get so caught up in those green eyes and his sexy smile that I'd let him take me the way he had.

God, what must he have thought of me? I'd let him drag me into a room and fuck me against the wall like a common whore. I may have left that room sated and satisfied, with the image of those eyes and his perfectly formed abs burned into my memory, but I can't let something like that happen again.

Walking into the services, I find the ladies' room and relieve myself, before grabbing some chocolate and a coffee to go. I'm back on the motorway within ten minutes, and I force myself to think of anything but that night.

I really can't wait to get to the little cottage I will be calling home for the foreseeable future. I've been told that I can arrange the furniture as I want, and I'm welcome to add any of my own touches to make the place feel more like my own.

The owners have also told me about a little boutique in town that sells handmade crafts they think I might like, and have left me a list of places they think I'll be interested in visiting, until I get my bearings and find my own way around.

Once I've unpacked, I've already decided to take the fifteen-minute walk down into Porthcurno town, just to see what's around. I also plan on seeing how far away my new job is from where I'll be living. A quick Internet search told me it's approximately a twenty-minute drive, but I want to see the route for myself so I can plan my journey in the morning. The last thing I want to do is follow the sat nav and then get stuck in roadworks or something similar. Being late isn't the kind of impression I want to make on my first day.

The minutes tick by, and soon I see a sign telling me I'm 21 miles outside of Porthcurno. I can feel the excitement building within me. I have so many things to be excited about, I'm not sure which one I'm looking forward to the most.

I'm both nervous and excited about starting at Creativity in Design. Even after speaking with Isobel several times, who has assured me the company and the people are friendly, and they are just as excited to meet me as I am about starting there. She told me she thinks of them as an extension of her family and is sure that, pretty soon, I will too.

I can see the sea on my right side as I drive along the winding road. I can tell I'm climbing, and when the sat nav announces I've arrived at my destination, I see the little cottage I now call home.

The place is even more beautiful than in the photos, and I make a mental note to thank my manicurist the next time I see her, although who knows when that will be. I pull my car onto the large driveway and turn off the engine. The owners told me they left a set of keys in a little 'hidey hole' on the porch, so when I'm out of the car and have climbed up the few steps, I seek it out, finding it exactly where they told me it would be.

I approach the front door and put the key in the lock, when I'm startled by a head that appears from around the side of the house.

"I'm sorry, I didn't mean to scare you. You must be Ellie?"

"Yes, that's right."

I watch when the head becomes a full person as he walks around to stand in front of me. I estimate him to be in his early thirties with dark brown, almost black hair. His eyes are almost as dark as his hair, and he is dressed in a casual polo neck and jeans.

"I'm Liam. I live next door. Erin and Pete said you were arriving today and asked that I stop by to make sure everything was okay. How was your drive down?"

"Yeah, it was okay, thank you. Long and boring, but okay."

"Daddy, where are you?"

"I'm up here, pumpkin."

I look towards the voice and see a small girl with curly blond hair peer cautiously around the corner of the house. When she sees her daddy, she hurries over, clinging to Liam's legs as she stares up at me. I'd put her at about four years old, and she is wearing a pink dress with matching ribbons in her hair. She has white sandals on her feet, which cover frilly ankle socks that remind me of when I was a little girl. I crouch down so I'm on her level and smile.

"Hi there, I'm Ellie. What's your name?"

"I'm Ewizabuf, but I wike Wizzy."

"Well, it's nice to meet you, Lizzy."

I hold out my hand and wait until the little girl comes around from behind her father's legs and takes it. I shake it gently, earning myself a little smile and a giggle from Lizzy, who is quickly scooped up into the arms of her father.

"Shouldn't you be with Mummy, baby girl?"

"Mummy said to come get you so we can go."

I watch the interaction between father and daughter and can't help but smile. I want to have that one day. Children have always been part of my plan. But I'm only twenty-one, so I know I have plenty of time for that. Not to mention I am nowhere near ready to be a mother.

"Sorry, I should get going. We're heading into town for a

late lunch. You're welcome to join us if you want. Maybe we could show you around a little?"

"Oh no, I couldn't intrude on your family time. Thank you anyway."

"You wouldn't be intruding. Hold on a second."

When he turns and peers around the corner, I watch him get the attention of someone—I assume his wife—before looking back at me. A few seconds later, a tall brunette joins us by my front door. If I had to use one word to describe her, it would be statuesque. She's easily pushing six feet tall and has long auburn hair almost down to her waist, which she's wearing in a long braid. Her eyes are a rich chocolate brown, and she's wearing blue jeans and a light cotton blouse. She's definitely a striking woman. I bet Liam gets told about how lucky he is all the time.

"Marnie, meet Ellie. She's going to be staying here while Erin and Pete are in Canada. I just invited her to lunch. Thought we could show her around a bit while we're in town."

"Oh, that would be lovely. Ellie, welcome to Porthcurno. It's a small town, but everyone is so friendly that I'm sure you'll fit right in."

I look at the three pairs of eyes that are all now looking at me expectantly. I know I should say no, go indoors and start unpacking so I can do the things I'd planned to do before tomorrow, but with the little girl looking at me the way she is, I know my afternoon isn't going to be spent as I originally hoped.

"Well, if you're sure you don't mind, it would be nice to see a bit of the town."

"Of course we don't mind. It'll be nice for me to have another woman to talk to. Liam, help Ellie unload her car before we go. Your things will be perfectly safe in the car, but we don't want to give anyone ideas now, do we?"

Liam hands off their daughter to his wife, and less than twenty minutes later, all my things are locked away in the house. I'm now walking into town with two people I have only just met, and I'm holding the hand of their little girl, who, it seems, has decided I'm her new best friend.

5

*I*t's almost seven by the time I get back to the house. Even though the afternoon wasn't what I'd planned, I have to admit, I did enjoy myself. Liam and Marnie took me to a little seafood place just across the road from the beach, where I ate some of the best garlic shrimp I've ever tried. It was so tasty I was tempted to ask for the recipe.

We then walked along the seafront, and they pointed out several other pubs and restaurants they like, and a few other places they thought I might be interested in. Marnie had been constantly speaking about how great it was to live in the town, and little Lizzy didn't leave my side from the moment we left the house.

Liam practically had to pry his daughter off me when we got back. The little girl was grizzly and rubbing her eyes, and I knew it was down to how tired she was. It's true what they say about sea air making you sleepy. Even though it's only early, I feel like I could just crawl into bed and sleep, but I still have too much to do.

Luckily, I only have two suitcases and three boxes to

unpack, so I'm hoping it won't take too long. I know I won't have time to do the trial run to work, so I'll just have to leave a little earlier in the morning to make sure I arrive on time.

I walk over to where I left my suitcases, grab one handle in each hand and drag them through to what will be my bedroom. I push the door with my hip, and my mouth drops open at the sight before me. I know the size of rooms can be deceptive in photographs, but the room I'm standing in now is enormous.

I have never slept in a dual aspect room before, but I have one now, all to myself. On one side of the room there are two French doors that lead out onto the porch, which has spectacular views of the town and the beaches below. On the other is a bay window that looks out onto green fields and has a bench seat built into it. I have seen films and read books that depict bench seats set into windows and have always loved the idea of having one.

There is a huge king-sized bed centred along the main wall, with built in wardrobes opposite. There is also a small dressing table and chair, and of all things, a chaise lounge next to the French doors. The room is decorated in creams and lilacs, and I begin to wonder if it is possible to fall in love with a room. It is stunning, and it's all mine.

Leaving my suitcases at the end of the bed, I walk through the rest of the house, seeing it is just as beautiful as I imagined it would be. The owners have even left me a couple of little care packages. The one I find in the kitchen includes the basics like tea, coffee, and sugar. I also find a loaf of bread in one of the cupboards and some milk and a bottle of wine in the fridge.

The second package is in the en-suite bathroom, and it consists of a new toothbrush, toothpaste, some shower gel, and shampoo and conditioner. There is also a little note from them saying they hope I enjoy staying there, and they are always available by email if I need anything.

I go back through to the living area and retrieve my phone from my bag. I pull up my email to send Erin and Pete a quick message to say thank you, when I see I've received an email from Isobel that was sent a little over two hours ago.

Furrowing my brow, I wonder why I didn't see it sooner, then remember what Liam said about the sketchy internet reception down in the town. The email must have come through when I reconnected to the 4G network that Liam mentioned got better the higher you went. I click on the email to open it, and read:

From: Isobel.Langley@creativityindesign.org.uk
To: Eleanor.Fox@myinternet.com
Subject: Tomorrow
Hi Ellie,
I hope this email finds you well.
When you arrive tomorrow, please can I ask you to park your car in the blue section, which is reserved for visitors. You will be assigned a parking space in the staff car park once you have received your ID badge and we know all your login credentials are set up and working.
Your start time is officially 9am, but I would appreciate it if you can try and arrive by 8:45, so we have time to sign you in. I shall meet you in reception and will then show you around the building and introduce you to the team.
I look forward to finally meeting you, Ellie, and hope you enjoy the rest of your Sunday.
Kind regards,
Isobel

I read the email several times, each time the smile on my face growing a little bigger. It really is happening. Tomorrow I will be starting my career in interior design.

After reading the email once more, I click out of it and compose a quick thank you email to Erin and Pete, before returning to my bedroom to unpack. As I remove each item of clothing and put them away, I carefully put together an outfit for my first day.

I've been told by Isobel that they aren't overly formal, but that smart/casual wear is expected. So, after going through my wardrobe several times, I finally decide on a pair of slim leg black trousers and a baby pink jacket with a white camisole underneath.

The trousers are of a length that I can wear either heels or flats, and seeing as I have a feeling I will be doing a lot of walking around tomorrow, I opt for a pair of plain black ballet flats to complete the outfit.

After laying out the clothes on the chaise lounge, I go through to the en-suite. I need to freshen up so I look my best tomorrow, so I flick on the shower and leave it so it can warm up. After finding towels, I step under the spray, and sigh deeply, relaxing as the hot water beats down my back.

Two hours later, I'm in bed. Everything is ready for the next day, and despite being nervous, I can't wait for tomorrow to come around. After setting my alarm for seven the following morning, I settle among the multitude of pillows and take a deep breath, before falling into an exhausted sleep.

6

---

*W*aking up to my alarm, I stretch my arms above my head and yawn loudly. For a moment, I forget where I am and sit bolt upright, taking in my surroundings. Several moments pass before I remember where I am, and that today I start my new job, and hopefully my new career in interior design.

Smiling widely, I jump out of probably the comfiest bed I've ever slept in and go through to the en-suite. After I've freshened up, I sit at the dressing table and open my makeup case, deciding that I will go for simple and classy with mascara, light nude eyes and pale pink lips.

When I'm happy with my face, I pull the elastic out of my hair and unwind the braid I put in the night before, before running my fingers through my brown locks. As I'd hoped, the braid has created a subtle wave in my hair that falls down around my shoulders.

Before getting dressed, I pick up my bag from where I dropped it the night before and put it on the bed, pondering exactly what I will need for the day. I drop in my hairbrush, lip gloss, and other feminine essentials before checking my keys are in there too.

When I'm sure I have everything, I approach the chest of drawers, grab some underwear and proceed to dress for the day. I am ready and raring to go in less than forty minutes and decide to head out. I know I will probably be mega early but seeing as I didn't get a chance to do a trial run yesterday, I have no idea where I'm going. I would rather be there early than risk leaving here a bit later, getting lost on my way there, and arriving late on my first day.

As I leave the house and lock up, I see Marnie walking down to her car. I give her a wave as she sees me and speaks.

"Morning Ellie. First day at the new job today, isn't it?"

"That's right," I reply as I walk to my car. "Heading out a bit early to make sure I'm not late."

"Good idea, although I think it's a pretty straight route from what you told me yesterday. You should find it no problem. Anyway, I'd best get going before Lizzy throws another hissy fit because we ran out of her favourite cereal. Good luck today."

"Thanks Marnie, I'll see you later."

We both climb into our cars, and I watch Marnie pull away before I start up the sat nav and program the address for the office. As it's rush hour, it states it will take approximately 35 minutes to reach work, and traffic is heavier than usual on my selected route.

Starting the engine, I put my hands on the steering wheel and pause for a moment. This is it. I am about to head out to start my first proper job. Hopefully it will be the job that will catapult me into the world of interior design, something I have wanted to do since I left school at sixteen.

Reversing off the drive, I point the car in the direction the sat nav tells me and pull away.

~

It's 8:10 when I arrive at the office. I easily find a parking space in the visitors' section and then sit in my car wondering when it will be okay to go inside. I managed to park in a space that has a clear view of the office I will soon be calling my second home.

It has a completely glass front with two hefty doors that open into a large foyer. I can see a second level mezzanine that looks down over the reception area, which has an intricate water feature on one of the walls.

Considering it isn't a large national company, it sure looks like one. First impressions are everything, and Creativity in Design has hit the nail right on the head. The place looks impressive, so I can only imagine what a client thinks when they drive up.

The minutes tick by, and soon it is 8:40. Deciding I've been sat here long enough, I grab my bag from the passenger seat and retrieve my keys from the ignition. When I'm standing outside the car, I take a breath and head towards the main entrance. Through the doors, I can see a tall redhead waiting at reception, who starts to approach me as I walk through the doors.

"Ellie?"

"That's right. You must be Isobel. It's nice to meet you."

I shake her outstretched hand and take in her appearance. She's wearing a sky-blue trouser suit, with a white blouse and black heels. Her red hair is worn straight and falls over her shoulders. She is a pretty woman who, like me, has gone for minimal make-up, and the smile she has on her face looks genuine.

"Nice to meet you too. Did you find the place okay?"

"Yes, no problem. This is a gorgeous building."

"Thank you, we all like it. Kyle and Kevin got lucky when they found this place. It was marked for demolition, and they were driving past one day and saw it. They thought it would be perfect to start up the business, and here we are."

I walk alongside Isobel as we approach the reception desk. We're greeted by a man in a dark blue suit and red and black striped tie. His dark hair is swept back off his face, and I catch the glint of a wedding ring on his left hand.

"Jamie, this is Eleanor Fox. She's joining us today. Can you arrange for someone to take her photo for her access pass please?"

"Sure thing, Miss Langley. I can take it right now if you have the time?"

Isobel looks at me, and I just nod and turn to Jamie.

"Where do you want me?"

I watch as Jamie opens one of the desk drawers and pulls out a small, handheld camera. He comes around the desk and walks over to stand by me and Isobel, indicating a plain white wall a few feet away.

"Over here is fine," Jamie says as I follow him over and stand with my back to the wall. "Say cheese."

I find myself smiling at Jamie's words just as he presses the button, then he moves the camera away so he can see the photo.

"Perfect," Jamie says with a smile. "Would you prefer Eleanor or Ellie on the pass?"

"Ellie, if that's okay?"

I look at Isobel, as if asking permission, who just holds her hands up.

"It's your pass, Ellie. You're the one who has to look at it every day, so it's up to you."

"Ellie it is then," Jamie says as he returns to the reception desk. "I'll have the pass ready for you in a few hours. I'll call Miss Langley when it's ready."

"Thank you, Jamie," Isobel replies. "And how many times, it's Isobel," she adds as she escorts me over to a bank of lifts.

"As you probably saw from the outside, we only have two levels. The ground floor is where most of the meeting rooms are, four in total, as well as one large conference room. We all work on the first floor. We have five full-time designers and two part-time who job share. Kyle is still very hands on with the design side of things, so he likes to keep tabs on what cases we have and how they're progressing. Some think he is micromanaging us, but he just wants to know what's happening in his own company, and personally, I think I would do the same if it were mine."

We step into the lift when it arrives and start up to the first floor.

"I think that's understandable," I reply. "I read up on the company when I was offered the position. I think if I had built a company from the ground up, I'd want to know what was going on too."

"Exactly. Kyle is out of town at the moment, so you won't meet him until later in the week, but Kevin is due in this afternoon. He's the one that deals with the business side of things, so he is the moneyman. His pet project right now is trying to get permission to put a gym down in the basement. It's just dead space at the moment, so he wants to do some-thing with it, and seeing as both him and his brother hit the local gym regularly, it seemed to be the best fit."

We are only in the lift for a few moments before the doors slide open, and we step out onto the mezzanine. I was right about the water feature on the far wall. It's an intricate pattern made of what looks to be metal and glass. Strategically placed fairy lights cause the water to shimmer as it makes its way down into the small pool at the base of the feature.

"That was another of Kevin's projects," Isobel says when she sees me staring.

"It's beautiful," I respond.

"Kevin will be happy to hear you say that. He's been toying with the idea of removing it. Hearing you like it, as someone new to the company, might just make up his mind to keep it."

Isobel begins to walk away, and I take one last look at the water feature before hurrying to catch up with her. We move past a few small offices before we come to a large glass door that is emblazoned with the Creativity in Design logo. Isobel puts her hand on the door before turning back to me.

"Ellie Fox, welcome to Creativity in Design."

7

---

*W*hat. A. Day.

I collapse onto the bed as I kick off my shoes. That must be one of the longest and most exciting days of my very short working life. I met so many people, whose names I know I'll forget by the time tomorrow comes around, if I've not forgotten already. I followed Isobel around all day, even getting to sit in on a last-minute meeting with a new client.

I hit the ground running when Isobel asked me if I minded taking some notes, even though it was my first day. I was only too happy to help, and I found my login credentials worked perfectly when Isobel showed me to my desk so I could type up the notes I took in the meeting.

I have a desktop computer for when I am onsite, and a tablet that doubles as a laptop when a keyboard is attached for when I need to accompany Isobel to offsite meetings. My desk is located just outside Isobel's office, and I have a clear view of the entire floor, including the offices reserved for Kevin and Kyle Brendan.

As Isobel said, I got to meet Kevin that afternoon. He's a tall man, well over six feet, with sandy blond hair that he wears cut short in the most recent style. I remember from his online bio that he is thirty-one years old, and the wedding ring on his left hand told me he was off the market, which I know must have broken the hearts of many women. The man is very easy on the eyes, so I know it won't be a hardship to see him from my desk every day.

Both Kevin and Isobel told me bits and pieces about the absent brother. Kyle Brendan is twenty-eight and has a good eye when it comes to interior design. He's able to tell at a glance whether something will work or not. They also told me he has a wandering eye for the opposite sex.

Both of them joked that I was just his type, and even though I was more than a little embarrassed by their words, I assured them I have no intention of letting anything happen with one of my bosses, no matter how much of 'his type' I might be.

The rest of the afternoon was pretty much Isobel showing me around the building, pointing out the ladies' bathrooms, the fire exits, and the large kitchen and break area. There were several microwaves and fridges, not to mention tea and coffee making facilities, along with a handy list that was stuck to the fridge detailing everyone's drink preferences.

Six large wooden tables were each surrounded by four chairs, and over at the far end, there were comfier chairs and a couple of sofas, all positioned around a large flatscreen TV. Isobel told me that Kevin and Kyle like the staff to relax on their breaks, so they try to make things as comfy as possible. Everyone must take a minimum of one hour for their lunch break, the only exception being for the people who work part-time, or if a shorter lunch has been approved by management.

Once Jamie called to say my access pass was ready, Isobel gave me some time to explore by myself. I was seriously impressed with what I saw, and I have a distinct feeling I am going to enjoy working there.

Isobel let me leave a little after 4pm, and on the way out, Jamie told me what parking space I had been allocated and pointed it out so I knew where I needed to go in the morning. After thanking him, I went into town to get some shopping done. The owners had left me the basics, but I needed some proper food. There was only so long I could survive on toast and sandwiches.

I unpacked what I bought, and now I'm stretched out on my bed, ready to sleep, and it's only just after 6pm. Knowing I will be doing just that if I stay where I am, I sit up and walk over to the dresser. After pulling out a t-shirt and yoga pants, I strip out of my work clothes and change.

After putting my hair up into a loose ponytail, I scoop out my phone from my bag, seeing I have several messages from various people wishing me luck, and one from Becky, asking me to call her when I get home.

I know I can't put off speaking with her forever. I also know I can't have this conversation without wine. I go through to the kitchen and open the fridge, pulling out the bottle that Erin and Pete left for me, checking out the label and wondering if they know they'd bought my favourite. I pour myself a large glass before going through to the living room, and as I stretch out on one of the sofas, I call Becky.

"Well, hello there, stranger. How was your first day?"

"Hey Bex. My first day went well, thank you. It's a lovely place. I think I'm going to enjoy working there."

"That's good to hear, Ellie. I worry with you being so far away."

I roll my eyes, something I seem to do every time I speak with Becky, and take a long drink of my wine.

"Becky, we've gone over this hundreds of times. I shall be fine. I'm a big girl. I know what I'm doing."

"Yeah, I guess you do," Becky says before pausing. "A bit like you knew what you were doing on Friday night. You little minx. I never knew you had it in you."

"Honestly? Neither did I. Hell, Becky, I didn't plan anything like that. I just wanted a fun night out, but then I saw him, looked into those gorgeous green eyes of his, and I just couldn't say no."

"Oh, I get that, Ellie. He looked hot. I swear I could see the sparks flying from across the room. You two generated some serious heat."

I take another mouthful of wine, feeling myself flush as I think back to what happened Friday night. I'd be lying if I said my mystery man hadn't played a part in my dreams the last couple of nights, and what dreams they'd been.

"Yeah, well, it was just one night. I had the fun time I was after, and now it's time to get serious about things. I really think I can make something of myself at this company, Becky. The people are great, the woman I'm working for, Isobel, is lovely, and the main boss—well, one of them anyway—is rather easy on the eyes, so no hardships so far."

"Sounds like you've landed on your feet, babe. What's the place like where you're staying?"

"The house is beautiful. I met the neighbours yesterday and they took me into town. We had lunch, and then a walk around. I'll send you some photos later. The view is wonderful."

"I can't wait to come down and see it. We'll have to arrange a weekend for me to visit when you're settled."

"Of course, I'd love that."

I chat with Becky for another ten minutes before we end the call. I'm pleased that I've finally talked with her about

Friday night, and truthfully, I don't know what I was worried about. There was no judgement from her, and now we've spoken about it, we have agreed not to bring it up again.

I lift the wine to my lips and realise I've polished off the glass, so I return to the kitchen for a refill. I scroll through the good luck messages, not surprised to see my parents haven't bothered to send me one. I have three from my brother, sent at various times throughout the day. I sip my wine as I walk into the bedroom and reply to his messages. He responds after a few minutes with a lot of emojis, which makes me smile.

Putting my phone on charge, I curl my legs beneath me and lean back against the pillows. Closing my eyes, I just listen, only now realising how quiet it is. Back home, as I lived just off a main road, there was always the noise of traffic, no matter what time of day it was. Right now, I can hear nothing but my own breathing. It's silent.

Now that I'm away from home, I know I need to find some way to fill my evenings. Having a quiet night in with a glass of wine is okay every now and then but doing it every night isn't really an option.

I'm about to grab my kindle from my laptop bag, when there is a knock at the door. Jumping up from the bed, I briefly glance at my reflection in the full-length mirror on the front of the wardrobe before I head out of the bedroom. I look through the peephole, opening the door when I see who it is.

"Hey Ellie, just thought I'd pop around and see how your first day went. I hope you don't mind?"

"No, of course not. Come on in."

I stand to the side and let Marnie enter, spotting the bottle of wine she holds in her hand.

"I thought you might like a little something after what I'm sure was a manic day for you. New faces, new work," Marnie says as she hands me the bottle.

"You read my mind. I've a bottle open so, if you don't mind, I'll pop this one in the fridge and get you a glass from the one I'm halfway through?"

I smile when Marnie laughs as we walk through to the kitchen.

"You're a girl after my own heart," she says as I pour her a glass of wine. "Erin and Pete really did a great job with this place," Marnie exclaims as we walk through to the living room. "I remember when they bought the house. It was a little run down, but it looks like they brought it back to life." She runs her hand across the back of one of the sofas. "I'm guessing it was all Erin. Pete was a lovely man, but he didn't know the first thing about soft furnishings or paint. Now, give him a hammer and some nails and he was a regular Mozart. He built that porch all by himself."

"They did a really good job," I say as I sip my wine. "I still can't quite believe they were willing to let me stay here. I thought I was going to have a hard job finding somewhere half decent down here, so when I was told about this place, I called, and they accepted," I explain before walking over to the door. "It's a nice evening, so how about we go and sit on the porch swing?"

Marnie nods and follows me to the door that leads us out onto the porch. We sit, and I sigh.

"I don't think I'll ever get used to this view."

"I know what you mean. Liam and I used to rent a little place down in the town. When I found out we were pregnant, we both decided that we wanted to stay close to the town, but we needed to find somewhere that wasn't right in the middle of things. When we saw the advert for the house next door, we weren't sure about it, but as soon as we saw the view, that was it. Regardless of what the house was like on the inside, we wanted that view. We put in an offer there and then and have been there for almost three years now. Best decision we ever made." We both go quiet for several minutes, just looking out over the sea before Marnie speaks, "So, how did your day go?"

Like I'd done on the bed earlier, I curl my legs underneath me and relay the story of my first day for what feels like the hundredth time today.

8

*S*o far, my first week has gone without a hitch. I've met almost everyone who works in the office, have even gone to lunch with a few of the girls, and tonight, they are taking me to a little cocktail bar five minutes from the office. I have a change of clothes in my bottom drawer, and I'm counting down the hours until 5pm comes so I can get changed and go out for a much-needed drink.

My week has been made up of shadowing Isobel, registering for the training courses that I need to do to qualify as a designer, and sitting in on meetings to help Isobel. Week one is almost out of the way, and today I get to meet Kyle Brendan, the other owner of Creativity in Design.

I'm not sure when he's coming in, but Isobel has told me it will be sometime this afternoon, which means sometime in the next four hours. With everything I've heard about him, I am excited to meet the man himself. The girls have described him using words like 'dreamy', 'super-hot', and my favourite, 'sexy as sin'.

I'm intrigued to know if they're right. Of course, everyone's taste in the opposite sex differs, but so far, all the girls in the office agree that the guy is off the charts attractive. Could Kyle Brendan be the one guy all the women want?

"Ellie, could you come in for a minute please," I hear Isobel call out, so I lock my computer and enter her office, seeing my boss hunting around on her desk as if she's lost something.

"Yes, Isobel?"

"The minutes from the Linden meeting. Did you put them on my desk like I asked? I can't seem to find them."

"They're in the red folder in your tray stack."

Isobel swivels her chair around to face the trays, putting her hand on the folder straightaway.

"I swear, I'd lose my head if it wasn't screwed on. Thank you, Ellie. I hear you're going out for drinks with a few of the girls tonight. Sounds like you're fitting in well. How has your first week been?"

"It's gone really well. Everyone has been so nice to me. I think I'm really going to enjoy it here."

"Well, that's good to hear. I think you've fitted in well, and the feedback I've had so far has all been positive, so keep doing whatever it is you're doing, and you'll be fine."

I smile at Isobel's words before I return to my desk. I unlock my computer and continue typing up the notes from our meeting that morning. I'm halfway finished when my screen flashes to indicate I have a personal message through the instant messaging service. Clicking on the icon, I see it's from Eliza, one of the other assistants, who is sat at the opposite end of the office. Opening it, I read:

Eliza F: Brace yourself. Mr Hot AF has just entered the building.

I grin widely, knowing that Eliza is best friends with Jamie on the reception desk. He's probably messaged her to let her know our elusive second boss is on his way up, and she, in turn, contacted me, and by the looks of all the heads that are now turning towards the main entrance, it isn't only me she's messaged. I swear every female in the office is craning their necks to see when he comes in.

I continue with my work while keeping one eye on the doors, pleased I'm able to multitask. When I see them swing open, I watch as a guy walks in, shaking hands with a few people as he passes by. Like his brother, he is over six feet tall with dirty blond hair and... Lord above, he is wearing a three-piece suit. I love guys who wear waistcoats with a suit. In my mind, there is nothing sexier than a man who can pull off a complete suit, and from the looks of it, Kyle Brendan definitely fits into that category.

He continues coming down the office, smiling at people as he passes them, but as he nears and turns his head in my direction, I stop typing and freeze. My breathing accelerates, and I feel myself begin to heat up as all too familiar green eyes lock onto my position. I see the moment recognition hits him as his step falters slightly and his eyes widen.

Crap. Shit. Fuck.

This can't be happening. How did my one-night stand, a man I am supposed to never see again, turn out to be my boss? How could I not know? Oh yeah, that's right, I never thought to ask his name as he fucked me against a wall and gave me a mind-blowing orgasm.

I force my eyes away as he gets closer, trying my hardest to hide behind my monitor. Maybe if I don't look at him, he won't be there? He'll simply vanish. Or, I'm going to wake up any minute now and it will all be a dream. Yes, that's what is going to happen. I am in some crazy dream, and the man standing by my desk right now isn't my one-night stand.

"Hi."

Even after the loud music that had been playing in the

44

club on Friday night, I would never forget that voice. Any doubts I had—and they had been minimal—that my boss and my fuck buddy were the same guy have vanished in that one simple word. Biting the bullet, I look up, seeing him peering down at me. His expression is unreadable, and that unnerves me a little.

"Hi."

It's all I can get out, not trusting my voice to expand any further on what I want to say. Hell, what do I want to say? *'Remember me? I'm the girl you fucked against a wall a week ago.'* Yeah, I'm sure that would go down well.

"Well, this is a pleasant surprise. I didn't expect to see you again."

Time to pull up your big girl pants, Ellie. He's just a guy. It was one night. You're both adults, live with it, girl.

"You and me both," I say with a nervous laugh.

"Kyle, it's nice to see you. How were your meetings?" Isobel says as she comes out of her office to stand by my desk. "Oh, of course. Kyle, this is Ellie Fox. She's my new assistant slash interior designer in training. Ellie, this is Kyle Brendan, our other boss."

"Thank you, Isobel. Ellie and I have met, and the meetings went very well thank you. I'll be in my office if you need me. I've a few calls I need to make. Nice to meet you, Ellie."

Despite my best efforts, I feel myself smile up at him, and a flush creeps to my cheeks when he smiles back. I can't take my eyes off him as he turns and walks across to his office. I inwardly groan when I realise his office is directly opposite my desk, giving me an unobstructed view of him every time he is there.

"Oh, I've seen that look before," Isobel says, getting my attention. "Don't go there, Ellie. Kyle is a great guy, but when it comes to women, he's got a reputation that you don't want to be part of. Trust me, I know."

I recognise the look on Isobel's face and don't need to ask what she means by that last comment. Something has clearly gone on between her and Kyle, and she is now warning me off him. What she doesn't know is that I have already gone there, but now I know I work for him I have no intention of going there again.

"Don't worry, Isobel, I don't plan on getting involved with anyone I work with."

Isobel peers down at me, giving me a look that tells me she is trying to figure out whether to believe me. When she turns and goes back into her office, I figure I have overcome that hurdle. Now all I have to do is figure out how I'm going to do my job with Mr One-Night Stand in my eyeline for the rest of the day. When I glance across to see him looking directly at me, I know it's not going to be easy.

9

*N*ow that I'm out of my work clothes, I can finally say the weekend has started. I'm in the ladies' room with three of the girls, all of whom have changed clothes, some going for jeans, others for skirts, and are now touching up either their hair or their makeup.

I have been looking forward to tonight ever since Eliza mentioned it earlier in the week. The place they are taking me to is just around the corner and, according to Mel, one of the other girls, it has the best cocktail menu for miles. They also have a good selection of light bites for people who want a snack with their alcohol.

"Did you girls get a load of Kyle today? I swear that guy gets hotter every time I see him and boy does he look good in a suit."

"You can say that again. Say, seeing as we're all girls together, no harm in asking. Have any of you ever been there?"

I listen as there are choruses of 'No' and 'I wish' followed by a lot of laughter and crude comments. When I'm the only one left to answer, I see they are looking at me expectantly.

"I only met the guy today, give a girl some time."

I laugh at my own words, and the rest of the girls join in. *Oh, if only they knew.* There is no way I am going there again, no matter how hot the guy looks in, and out of, a suit.

Within ten minutes we are all finished getting ready and are heading out of the building. Eliza leads the way to the cocktail bar, which I am surprised to see is literally around the corner. Mel manages to snag us a booth right by the bar while Beth goes and orders our first round of drinks. We've all agreed to do rounds tonight, which I am more than okay with.

It's been a while since I went out with a group of girls. Back home, there is only really Becky that I go out with. Our nights out are fun but predictable. We always wind up going to the same places, drinking the same drinks. With the exception of last week, which I would rather forget, I've never done anything fun like this before.

When Beth returns to our table, a waiter follows her, holding a tray that contains two pitchers of a bright orange liquid. Beth squeezes in next to me as the waiter places the pitchers on the table, along with four glasses.

"Ladies, I thought we would start simple tonight. Sex on the Beach."

A cheer goes up from the table as Mel pours each of us a glass of the orange cocktail, and we all pick up our glass and drink. The cool liquid slides smoothly down my throat, and I decide this is just what I need right now. I didn't plan on getting drunk tonight, but now that I'm here and I've taken my first sip, I have a feeling that what I originally planned might just go out the window, and it could be exactly what the doctor ordered.

~

Two hours later, it's my round, and we are on our seventh and eighth pitchers. This time, it is Blue Lagoon and I am starting to feel the effects of the alcohol, even though it's only 7:30pm. I've practically been laughing non-stop for the last thirty minutes, my head is a little fuzzy, and my coordination isn't the best, which is why I'm taking the pitchers to our table one at a time, just to make sure they both make it in one piece.

By the time I'm seated again, the drinks have already been poured, and Mel turns to me.

"So, how are you enjoying the job so far, Ellie?"

"Honestly, I'm loving it. This is my first proper job as I'm straight out of Uni. I've had to move so far away from home, but I think it's the best decision I ever made."

"Yeah, and you got the best seat in the whole damn office," Eliza says as she sucks her drink through a straw. "I don't think I'd get any work done if I could see Kyle all day, or Kevin for that matter, but he's off the market."

I fight the urge to roll my eyes. What is everyone's obsession with this man? Sure, he seems like a nice guy, a great dresser, and hotter than hell, but he is still just a guy. Nothing special. Nothing at all. I take a sip of my drink and realise I'm trying to convince myself that Kyle Brendan is just a regular guy, when he is anything but.

As the other three continue their hero worship of our boss, I excuse myself to go to the bathroom. When I've finished my business, I wash up and stand in front of the mirror, taking in my reflection. Deciding I need more lipstick, I retrieve it from my bag and apply it to my lips, smacking them together to even out the colour.

After fluffing my hair and flicking it over my shoulders, I leave the bathroom to return to the girls, stopping suddenly when I see a familiar figure at our table. He's discarded his suit jacket, but he is still wearing the waistcoat, and now has the sleeves of his shirt rolled up to the elbows, just like he did when I first met him.

I let my eyes move down his body. The white shirt and waistcoat fit his torso perfectly and taper down to a slim waist. I continue down, and I'm mesmerised by the way the light grey material hangs from his hips and curves around his perfectly formed backside.

This man is my boss, and I am his subordinate. I know it's wrong, but I'm not blind. Even I can admit he is hot, and truth be told, I would probably be thinking like this even if today *was* the first time I met him. Yet somehow, the fact that I have already been with him makes my lusting over him seem wrong.

I remain rooted to the spot as the three girls chat with Kyle. When he speaks, they hang on his every word, something I have never understood. Then again, after the way he spoke to me last Friday night, I know how seductive his voice sounds. I also know how filthy his words can be, so I can't really blame the girls for being spellbound when he speaks.

Right now, I'm torn between leaving them to it or growing a pair and walking over to them as if nothing ever happened between Kyle and me. I'm leaning towards the first option, when Mel spots me and calls my name. Everyone at the table turns to look at me, including Kyle.

When those eyes lock onto mine, damn if my body doesn't begin to betray me. Again. Right now, I'm having the same reaction to him that I had last week, and just like then, I'm not sure if it's down to the alcohol or just the presence of the man.

Knowing I can't run now, I pull back my shoulders and

walk as confidently as I can in four-inch heels over to the table, reclaiming my seat next to Mel. I spot two pitchers of what looks like Margarita, which wasn't there when I left, as well as the Blue Lagoons I bought.

"Ellie, we were beginning to think you'd abandoned us. I hope you like tequila because Kyle bought us some Margaritas."

"Thank you," I say as I turn to him, seeing him smiling at me.

"You're welcome, Ellie. The girls here were just telling me how much you have enjoyed your first week with us at Creativity."

I take a moment before responding, and just look at him. He doesn't seem to have any issue with what went on between us. If he can act like nothing happened, then so can I.

"I have. Let's hope it continues."

"I'm sure it will, We're like one big happy family. Aren't we, girls?"

Each of the girls respond with an affirmative nod, and each has a dreamy look on her face; a look Kyle is either ignoring or is oblivious to. Somehow, I doubt a guy who looks like him is unaware of the affect he has on women. He read me like a book last week, so I find it impossible to believe he doesn't know these girls are all crushing on him right now, and every time they set eyes on him.

"Hey Kyle! Get your ass over here!"

Everyone looks over when we hear someone shout Kyle's name, seeing a few of the guys from the office waiting by the bar.

"That's my cue, ladies. Enjoy the rest of your night, and I'll see you all bright and early on Monday."

With those final words, Kyle walks off, and all eyes,

including mine, fall to his backside. It isn't until he's with the other guys that we all pick up our drinks and drain each glass in turn, before Mel speaks.

"Did it suddenly get hot in here, or is it just me?"

10

*W*hen I walked into the office today and saw her sat outside Isobel's office, it felt like someone had poured a bucket of ice-cold water over me and then punched me in the gut for good measure. I knew we had taken on another assistant. My brother had handpicked her for the interview himself. I'd known her name was Eleanor Fox, and that she was the type of enthusiastic we love at Creativity in Design, but that had been it.

It never occurred to me that the girl I took so roughly against a wall last week would be the same girl starting at my company. The possibility was so remote, it never even entered my mind. I mean, why would it? My company is on the south coast. I was in Bristol last week, and most of this week, and I didn't bother to get her name whilst I fucked her, so the connection wasn't a logical one.

I hope I managed to cover my shock at seeing her there, at least better than she had anyway. I saw the moment she recognised me. Her blue eyes widened, and she gripped the edge of her desk a little too tightly. Before I knew what was happening, I was walking right up to her and saying, 'hi.'

With her long brown hair and baby blue eyes, I found myself drawn to her, just like I had been that night. Now, as I watch her enjoying the Margaritas I bought for her and some of the other girls from the office, I'm struck by just how beautiful she really is.

I didn't go out last week expecting to get any kind of action. I took a couple of prospective clients out for a meal and a few drinks and somehow wound up in the nightclub. I planned on staying for one drink and then going back to my hotel, but as soon as I laid eyes on her, I knew I would be staying longer than I initially intended.

She was drinking a brightly coloured cocktail and was dancing and laughing with her friend. She was wearing a tiny black dress with silver fuck me heels that made her legs look like they went on forever. If there is one thing I love on a woman, it's her legs. Oh, don't get me wrong, I'm a boobs guy too—I mean, aren't we all—and hers are certainly more than a handful. But legs, that's what gets my attention.

I let my mind drift back to how it felt when those legs were wrapped around my waist as I pumped into her. How she tightened around me; how her body trembled in my arms when I brought her to orgasm.

I have never been with a girl as responsive as she was that night, and I can't help but wonder if she is the same with every guy she's with, or if it was just me. I know I shouldn't be thinking things like this. She was a one-night shag. A bit of fun while I was away from home. Nothing more. But even now, as I watch her laugh and drink with the other girls, I can feel my cock beginning to pay attention, which is the last thing I need, especially with the company I'm currently in.

"Hey Kyle, who's the new girl?"

I'm jolted back to reality when I hear a voice talking to

me, and turn to see Simon, one of the designers, looking between me and the girls.

"Oh, that's Ellie. She's Isobel's new assistant and our new trainee."

"Ah right. It's about time we had someone new around the office. She's a looker. Might try my luck with that one. You reckon I'm in with a shot?"

All I can do is look at the guy and try to rein in my territorial instincts. I have no idea where they have come from, or why I am suddenly feeling this way, but when I listen to him talking about making a play for Ellie, and remember that my cock was inside her only last week, I can only think of one thing.

Mine.

"I don't know, mate. I think I heard Kev mention she's spoken for."

Why the hell did I say that? I have no idea whether she is spoken for or not. I'm guessing not, considering what happened between us, but I don't know for sure. Why didn't I just tell him about the rule against interoffice dating and steer him away? Now that I think about it, why the hell did I put that stupid rule in place?

Even though I have no plans to pursue Ellie further than I already have, the thought that it's against the rules sucks big time. Not pursuing her because it is my choice is one thing, but not pursuing her because of a stupid rule I implemented only six months ago, is another.

Is it too late to abolish it? No, that would be stupid, and leave me open to all sorts of complaints and ridicule from the staff. I will just have to learn to live with Ellie working in the office, in a position where I can clearly see her from my desk. Every time I'm there.

I have a feeling I'm going to have a permanent hard-on

from now on. There is no way I am going to be able to look at her and not think about how it felt to be inside her. Knowing how warm and tight she was when I thrusted into her.

Having knowledge of how she looks under her clothes is going to be another problem. I saw, touched and tasted her breasts as the firm mounds of flesh bounced up and down while I fucked her. I know how soft and creamy her skin is, and it's going to be a proverbial kick in the teeth that I can't see it all again every time I look at her.

I know I need to switch my attention back to the people I agreed to come out for a drink with, but it is hard with her so nearby. I can practically smell her perfume, having caught the scent when she returned to the table. I figure it's just my already active imagination kicking up a notch, or maybe I really can smell it. Either way, it's a distraction I could really do without right now, but I have a feeling this particular distraction is going to be around for a long time, and isn't that just a swift kick in the teeth.

11

---

*I*t's a little after midnight when I get back home. I am closer to drunk than I am sober, but I'm still able to walk in a relatively straight line, if that line includes several left and right turns.

I collapse onto the sofa and kick my shoes off, letting them hit the floor with a thud as I release a long sigh.

I can't quite believe the day I've just had. I know it's a cliché, but of all the offices in all the world, he had to walk into mine. Well, technically it's his, but the saying still applies. I was sure I was imagining things when he walked into the office, convincing myself it couldn't possibly be the same guy.

However, when he stopped by my desk and I looked up into those same bright green eyes that had captured my attention so fiercely last week, I knew it was really happening. I now work for the same guy whom I let fuck me stupid against a wall in the back of a nightclub after speaking only a few sentences.

God, what must he think of me?

Initially, I hoped he wouldn't recognise me, and when I

first saw him, I wasn't sure he knew who I was. You could call it denial. But any doubts I may have had were put to rest in the bar after work. The way he looked at me told me he knew exactly who I was, but I couldn't tell whether he was pleased about it or pissed. His expression was unreadable, and he gave nothing away in the way he spoke to me.

I fling my arm over my eyes as I lie there in the darkness, realising my job could now be in jeopardy. Sleeping with the boss is one of my hard limits, and something I promised myself I would never do. Even though I didn't know who he was at the time it happened, it doesn't change the fact that I did it, and him, and I've given him ammunition to use against me, if he is that kind of guy.

Everyone raves about Kevin and Kyle, saying how great they are to work for and how brilliantly they treat their staff. I just hope what happened won't affect our working relationship. So we had a one-night stand, big deal. If he can live with it, then so can I.

I hope.

Forcing myself into a sitting position, I swing my legs around, cursing when my ankle connects with the coffee table. Making a mental note to move the offending object the next day, I get to my feet, and once the room stops spinning, I head towards the bedroom, stopping when there is a knock at the door.

I furrow my brow and check my watch, seeing it is almost half past midnight. What could Marnie and Liam want at this time? Have I left my car lights on? No, that can't be it as my car is still parked at work, waiting for me to collect it sometime tomorrow. I'm tempted to ignore whoever it is and just crawl into bed, but when there is a second knock, I walk over, and without checking, open the door.

I fight to hide my surprise at seeing Kyle Brendan

standing on my doorstep. He is still wearing the waistcoat, but it is now unbuttoned. The shirt sleeves are still rolled up, and damn it he still looks good enough to eat. When you add in the ruffled hair, eyes that are still bright, even at this time of night, and the uncertain look on his face, I'm amazed I'm not a puddle on the floor.

"Mr Brendan, what are you doing here?"

I watch as his expression changes from uncertain to what I can only describe as amused as he gives me a half smile.

"I think we're past the formal stage, Ellie. You can call me Kyle."

"Okay, Kyle, but that doesn't answer my question. What are you doing here?"

I may have a few drinks swimming in my system, but I haven't drunk enough to make me ambivalent to him being here. Turning up on my doorstep at almost one in the morning isn't normal boss behaviour, and I have to remember that he is my boss. No matter how attracted to him I am right now.

"I wanted to talk to you and didn't get a chance in the bar."

I fold my arms across my chest and lean against the door-frame. I have to admit that I'm intrigued about what he wants to say to me that can't wait until we are back in the office on Monday.

"And this couldn't wait until Monday? It's almost 1am, and I was about to go to bed." As soon as I say the words, I realise how that must have sounded to him. "Not that I'm insinuating I want to go to bed with you, I mean. I didn't want that to sound like…"

When I see the smirk on his lips, I'm tempted to close the door in his too handsome face and just leave him out there, but something stops me, and I'm not sure what it is.

"I know what you mean, Ellie, and I know it's late, but I

don't think you want what I have to say to possibly be over-heard in the office. Can I come in please?"

This isn't a good idea. Having him on my doorstep means I can close the door and keep him out and away from me. Inviting him in means he is in my home, amongst my things. Suddenly, what was meant to have been a one-night stand, never to be seen of or heard from again, is coming back to bite me in the ass.

"I don't think that's a good idea, Kyle. It's late, and you're my boss. If anyone was to hear…"

"Who would find out? As far as I know, no one else from work lives around here, and unless you go and shout it around the office on Monday, something I won't do by the way, I think we're safe. Please, Ellie, I just want ten minutes, and then I'll go."

In that moment, I am torn between my heart and my head. I trust myself to not let anything happen between us again, but my heart is telling me to jump him and let him make me feel what he did last week. I have to work with this man. Knowing I have fucked him once already is bad enough, but that was before I knew who he was. It is completely different now. The way he is looking at me, almost pleading with me, wears away my resolve to keep him at arm's-length.

"Fine, you've got five minutes."

Against my better judgement, I step aside and let him enter. As I close the door, I watch him take a few steps into the room and look around the living area. I silently thank God I closed the bedroom door that morning. The last thing I want is for him to see my bedroom. Although, I have already put the idea of going to bed into his head with my earlier comment, one I am now kicking myself for saying.

"You have a lovely place."

"Thank you. I'm renting it from the family of a friend of mine. What do you want to say, Kyle?"

I want to get this over with, sooner rather than later. I have already decided I'm not going to invite him to sit down. Rude, maybe, but I am in self-preservation mode, and I don't want him getting too comfortable in my home. Especially not at one in the morning, when we've both been drinking and just being this close to him is sending my system into overload, something I am trying my hardest to ignore.

"Straight to the point," he says as he turns to face me. "Can we sit down?"

"I'd rather not. Anything you say can be said standing up."

He widens his stance and puts his hands in his pockets. I can't help it, my eyes drop down, and then straight back up when I see a tell-tale bulge below his waistline. My eyes connect with his, and I know he can tell I've seen his reaction to me—at least, I'm assuming the prominent hard-on he's doing nothing to hide is because of me.

"Okay. I just wanted to let you know that I won't let what happened affect us working together."

"I'm pleased to hear that."

"And I also promise to keep what happened just between us. I understand you're new to the company and don't want to give the wrong impression to the other guys in the office."

"Whoa, hold on a minute. What do you mean, 'give the wrong impression'?"

"Well you did kind of throw yourself at me, Ellie, and I wouldn't want the other guys to think you were, for want of a better word, easy."

I can't figure out if he is just being his usual self or if he is deliberately trying to get a reaction from me, but if he isn't, he sure as hell is going to get one.

"Now you just hang on a minute. I didn't throw myself at you. You're the one who took us into that office, I just followed."

Kyle takes his hands out of his pockets and folds his arms across his impressive chest. His expression is amused again, and I can tell he is enjoying this.

"As I recall, Ellie, you're the one who came up to me. I didn't approach you. You're also the one who asked me where I wanted to take you. I might have walked you into that room, but you initiated the encounter."

Damn it, he's right. I was the one to go over to him, with Becky's encouragement. I need to have a serious word with my friend the next time I speak to her. I need someone else to blame for this mess other than myself.

"Whoever initiated it, it doesn't matter, because no one else will ever know and it won't happen again."

I fold my arms and instinctively take a step away from him when he moves forward. When he takes another step, I find my back against the wall, and there's only a few inches between us. My breathing has picked up, and I know my cheeks are flushed. I just hope he hasn't noticed.

He drops his arms to his sides, and his head tilts slightly as he just looks at me. My eyes drop when his tongue darts out to lick his lips, and when I look up again, I see his eyes have darkened.

My insides clench deliciously, and I know I need to put some distance between us, and above all else, I can't let him touch me. If he does, I know I won't be able to put a stop to anything that may come after it. No matter how much I wish it wasn't true, my attraction to Kyle, and my desire to take him to bed, is undeniable.

"Are you sure it won't happen again, Ellie, because your body is saying otherwise."

I take a deep breath, which comes out in short pants as he inches closer. He isn't touching me, yet I can feel him all over me. Is it because I'm replaying the memory of last week in my head as I look at him? Or is it because his presence is so consuming that just being in the same room as him can cause me to react so strongly?

Am I sure it won't happen again? I want to say yes; want to shout it from the rooftops, but right here and now, in this moment, I know it would be a lie. If he touches me, I will throw myself at him. There is no two ways about it. Part of me wants him to touch me, just so I will have a reason to wrap my arms around his neck, lean in and press my lips to his. There is no way I am going to make the first move this time, no matter how much I want to climb his body like a climbing frame.

Clearing my throat, I find my voice as I fumble for the door latch and open it.

"Yes. Now I think you should go if you've said what you wanted to say."

I breathe out as the cool air from outside hits my heated skin, and I'm pleased that I am now able to put some space between us.

"Okay, I'll go, but there is more I want to say. Keep your afternoon free on Monday, Ellie. Kevin might have hand-picked you for the interview, but I never got a chance to meet you properly or test your skills. I'll send Isobel an email to let her know."

I don't miss the change in the tone of his voice. He's gone from soft and seductive to all business in two seconds flat. But his eyes are still boring into me. I know that whatever this thing is between us isn't over.

I nod in response to his words as he steps past me and out into the darkness, my eyes on his back as he walks away.

12

*W*ell, that was an interesting evening.

What compelled me to go back to the office after having drinks with the guys, find her personnel file, get her address, and then get a taxi over there, I have no idea. But I'd done it, and I think it's fair to say her reaction and our subsequent conversation didn't go as I thought it would.

If I'm honest with myself, I had no idea what I'd been expecting. Once I arrived at her place, I stood outside her door for five minutes contemplating whether I was doing the right thing in being there. I eventually told myself to grow a pair and knocked on the door.

When she didn't answer, I thought she may have already been in bed, and my mind went straight to the gutter, a place it seems to be permanently since I bumped into her again. I knocked a second time and decided that if she didn't answer this time, I would just leave her alone. Thankfully, the door swung open, and her shocked expression told me I was the last person she was expecting.

It was clear she was hesitant to let me inside. She did

eventually, but even then, she didn't let me sit down. Her defences went up almost straightaway when she folded her arms across her chest, and the horrified look she gave me when she realised she had been the one to initiate our tryst last week amused me no end.

But the one thing that got my blood pumping more than it already had been, was her reaction when she realised I was hard behind my trousers. I saw the pretty pink flush creep into her cheeks, and she was unable to hide the acceleration of her breathing. I affect her. Of that I have no doubt. And as soon as I realised that piece of information, I found I wanted to get closer to her.

It took everything in me not to reach out and touch her. My fingers itched to feel her soft skin again, and it took a monumental effort to keep my hands by my sides. When I licked my lips, hers parted and mimicked the action, and if I had to guess, I'd say she hadn't realised she'd done it.

I could tell she was fighting her attraction just as much as I was, and neither of us were willing to make the first move. I have a feeling this thing between us is going to come down to a battle of wills. Neither one of us wants to back down, but sooner or later, one of us will have to, and what was supposed to have been a one-night thing will turn into something completely different.

13

"*I* promise you, big brother, everything is going great. The people are great, the job is great, the house is great."

"Yeah, yeah, I get it. Everything is great."

I laugh at my brother's words as I wander down the street. After I showered and dressed this morning, I got a taxi to the office to retrieve my car, and then decided to come into town for a few hours to explore. I came down with Marnie and Liam the weekend before, but I haven't really had much time to look around by myself.

"So, when can I come and visit?" Eric asks me as I spot a little boutique shop across the street.

"You and Cammie are welcome anytime."

"It will just be me. I finally kicked Cammie to the kerb."

I stop in my tracks.

"Seriously? You and Cammie are through? What did Mum and Dad say?"

"Oh, Mum did her usual disapproving look and shook her head but didn't actually say anything. Dad just told me that I should rethink my decision as Cammie comes from the kind of family I should try and get on with as it would only improve my standing in the area, and by my standing, he meant theirs."

I shake my head as I carry on walking. That is just typical of our parents. Not bothered that their son has finally found a pair of balls and ended a relationship he hadn't wanted to be part of in the first place. All they care about is their social status, and what the breakup will do to them.

"You know what they're like, Eric. I'm just happy you finally ditched her. Now you can go find someone who you really want to be with."

"Yeah, imagine what Mum and Dad would say to that. If I brought home someone who I really wanted to be with, Mum would probably have a heart attack and Dad would disown me."

As much as I hate to admit it, Eric is right. Apart from a few of his closest friends, I am the only one who knows my brother is gay. He doesn't hide the information from anyone, other than our parents, but neither does he shout it from the rooftops. Eric likes to be discreet where his sexuality is concerned, but I know that when he does find the person he wants to be with, there is no way he will hide it from anyone, including our parents.

I check before I cross the road, pausing outside a boutique.

"You'll meet the right person eventually, big brother, then Mum and Dad will have no choice but to accept them, and you, for who you are."

"Yeah, I guess you're right. Love you, sis."

"Love you too, bro, now get back to work."

"Yeah, yeah, slave driver."

Eric ends the call, and I drop my phone into my bag before I push open the door to the boutique. I love places like this. The rails are full of clothes, but not your usual, everyday clothes that you find in most chain stores. Each piece looks unique. Not one item is the same as another, even though patterns are similar.

I walk over and start to look through one of the rails, pulling out a black sheath dress that is covered in red cherries. The fabric is soft and silky, and I can only imagine how much it costs as there is no price tag on it.

"That dress would look great on you."

I turn as a woman, who I assume to be one of the sales assistants, walks towards me. She is wearing a dress similar to the one I am holding, but hers is covered in sunflowers and looks great on her. Of course, this woman has the perfect figure for this style of dress, as well as the height, so I should hardly be surprised.

"It's really pretty, very similar to yours."

"They're by the same designer. She's a local. In fact, she makes quite a few of the pieces we sell here. We have this dress with various designs, but this is the only one we have with the cherry, so it would be one of a kind, so to speak."

"One of a kind means expensive, I'm guessing."

The assistant laughs and takes the dress out of my hands.

"You'd be surprised. Our prices are very reasonable when compared to other places in the area. Why don't you look around, see if there is anything else you like, and I'll take this into one of the fitting rooms so you can try it on."

"Thank you."

I turn back to the rail and flick through the items one by one. When nothing else catches my eye, I move on to the next. After less than ten minutes, as well as the cherry dress, I have picked up another dress, two skirts, and three blouses.

Each item can be dressed up for work or a night out or dressed down for everyday casual. Each item is gorgeous, and

I have no clue how much any of it costs. I am about to put some of it back when the assistant comes over after serving another customer.

"Looks like you've had fun."

"Yeah, I think I've gone a bit overboard."

"Nonsense," the assistant says as she comes to stand next to me before she begins to lead me over to one of the fitting rooms. "You go and try all that stuff on, I shall see what I can do about the cost. I'm sure we can reach an agreeable price."

Once I'm inside, the assistant closes the door and I slide across the lock. This place is so strange. I have never been in a store that has no prices on the products, and the price is agreed upon when paying, at least not here in the UK.

After hanging up the items on the rail, I try each one on, and by the time I've got to the cherry dress, I've all but decided that no matter what the price I will be buying all the items. The fabrics are so gorgeous. The skirts skim my thighs and float around my knees. Both dresses give me curves I haven't seen in a long time, and even I think I look hot.

Five minutes later, I'm back in my own clothes and heading out of the fitting room. I hand all the items over to the assistant, who is standing by the till.

"So, what are you having?"

"I really shouldn't, but everything is so lovely. I want it all."

The assistant smiles at me and retrieves some tissue paper from under the counter, then she proceeds to fold each item and place it in the centre of the paper.

"I thought you might. There are so many lovely pieces in here."

"My bank balance isn't going to like me much, but I can't resist."

"Oh, I don't know about that. I'm sure it can handle £125."

"Really? Only £125? Don't you need to get confirmation from the owner or something? Surely that isn't enough for all of this."

"I am the owner, honey, so I can charge whatever I like." I grin as the assistant/owner continues to wrap my purchases. "You're new in town, aren't you? I don't think I've seen you before. I'm Chloe."

"Yeah, I moved here last week for a new job. I'm staying at Pete and Erin's place. Nice to meet you, Chloe, I'm Ellie."

I wander around the store as my purchases are wrapped and packed, and glance at a pair of black and red heels that would look great with the cherry dress, but I refuse to buy them, on this trip anyway.

"Oh, I love Pete and Erin. I'm going to miss them. Congratulations on the new job though. Where are you working?"

"I'm an assistant at Creativity in Design."

"The one owned by the Brendan brothers?"

"Yeah, that's the one. You know it?"

I watch as the assistant continues wrapping my purchases, but now there is a little less finesse in her actions and a little more purpose. So much so that she tears one of the pieces of tissue paper, then curses under her breath as she grabs another sheet from under the counter and tears that piece too.

"Is everything okay? You seem a little upset."

"Oh, sorry. It's just that I've got history with the Brendan brothers. It's been years; I should really let it go. Anyway, here are your items. Will you be paying with cash or card?"

I let the quick change of subject go as I hand over my debit card and enter the PIN, but my curiosity is definitely piqued. What happened between her and the Brendan brothers that could cause such a strong reaction in her?

"There you go. I hope you'll come back soon. I saw you eyeing up those shoes over there."

And just like that, things are back to normal. Whatever upset her is now gone and she is back to the same woman she'd been when I walked into the shop. I take my new clothes, now all together in a bright pink shopping bag, and thank her before I turn and leave the store.

Checking my watch, I see it's almost two in the afternoon. I'm not ready to go home, and the reasons for that are twofold. One, I haven't seen enough of the town yet, and two, the smell of Kyle's aftershave still lingers in the air in the living room.

When I woke that morning, a slight headache dulled my senses for the first few minutes. But the more I awoke, the more prominent the scent was, and the memory of his visit last night came flooding back. I still can't quite believe he came round. Even more so, I can't believe I actually let him in my home.

It's going to be interesting at work on Monday. I know we came close to going at it right there in my hallway. I doubt we would have made it to the bedroom. I was torn between wanting him to touch me, just to feel his hands on me again, and maintaining the boss/employee relationship we now have. That is one line I don't want to cross; had promised myself I will never cross, but with Kyle, it's proving to be harder than I thought.

What went on between us should have been for one night only. Meet, fuck, and leave. That's it, nothing else. I was never meant to see him again, let alone work for the guy. Seeing him every day wasn't part of the plan, but I'm stuck with it, so I need to try and keep him at a distance if I am going to get any work done, and also maintain a strictly working relationship with him.

But he is so damn hot. No man should look as good as him, and when he wears the full three-piece suit, he looks like he's just stepped off the pages of GQ magazine. The man can put most professional models to shame with his looks, and I'm sure he'd make a small fortune if he ever decided to switch careers.

I can feel my pulse picking up speed, and all I'm doing is thinking about him. If I'm going to keep things professional, I need to stop thinking of him as a sexual object and start thinking of him as my boss; someone who is unattainable and off limits. Which would be easier said than done if I hadn't already sampled the goods.

Releasing a frustrated sigh, I continue down the road until I come to a little diner that Marnie and Liam pointed out the week before. As if on cue, my stomach growls. I smile as I step inside, hoping food will take my mind off the man who gave me the best sex of my life.

14

"*M*orning Ellie. How was your weekend?"

I smile at Jamie as I cross the foyer, pausing by the reception desk.

"It was lovely, thank you, Jamie. How was yours?"

"Great thanks. Chloe and I took the kids to their grandparents for the weekend so we could have some time together. It was our five-year anniversary."

"Oh, that's lovely. Congratulations."

"Thank you. We love the kids to bits, but it's nice to have some adult time every now and again."

I give Jamie a little wave as I continue to the lifts, walking out onto the first floor a few moments later. When I get to my desk, I am surprised to see Isobel isn't in yet, but a quick glance up tells me the Brendan brothers are. They are both huddled in Kevin's office, hunched over the desk looking at what appears to be floor plans, probably for a new client.

Both men have discarded their suit jackets and are wearing shirts with their ties tossed over their shoulders, so they won't get in the way. Now that I can see them together, it

73

is clear they are brothers. In fact, unless you knew otherwise, you would be forgiven for thinking they were twins. The resemblance between them is striking, something I didn't notice before. It's only now, seeing them side by side, that I wonder why I hadn't started to get suspicious the first time I saw Kevin.

Turning my attention back to my computer, I log in to my email account, seeing a message from Isobel saying she won't be in today for personal reasons, but she has sent me some work to keep me going and should be back in the office tomorrow.

I see several other emails from my boss, each relating to a different account she has been working on, with instructions telling me what she wants me to do for each one. *Well, at least I won't be stuck for something to do,* I think to myself as I begin to download and save the documents Isobel has sent me.

I spend the next thirty minutes organising my day to ensure I manage to fit everything in. When I hear an office door open, I look up to see Kevin walking over to me. Even though it isn't 9am yet, he looks seriously stressed over something.

"Ellie, I'm so glad to see you're here. Isobel won't be in today, she's dealing with a personal matter, but I understand she has sent you your work for the day?"

"Yes, she has. I've just been organising it, so I don't miss anything."

"Right, well I'm sorry but all your organisation is needed elsewhere. Kyle and I have been working on a project, and it seems the client hasn't been very forthcoming with the information we asked for, so all the work we've done so far has been for nothing, unless you can help us salvage some of it. You up for the challenge?"

I listen to Kevin's words, pleased that he thinks I am good enough to help them out, but at the same time, I am a little apprehensive at working so closely with Kyle. Realising that this could be a great chance to prove what I can do, I push aside my trepidation and stand.

"You bet," I say, and Kevin smiles.

"Good. Now I know you're new here, but you've impressed me so far. The updates I've had from Isobel have been very encouraging, especially the way you prioritise your work, and your organisation. I think you'll be fine with this."

"I appreciate the confidence you have in me, Kevin. What is it you need me to do?"

"Well, there are a few things, but first thing's first. I've been here since half six and haven't had my first cup of coffee yet."

"Oh, I can get that for you," I say as I pick up my own mug from my desk. "I was going to make myself one anyway."

"No, I'll get them," Kevin says as he takes the mug from out of my hand and turns to his office. "Kyle."

I watch as he calls to his brother and holds up my mug, receiving an approving nod in response before Kevin turns back to me.

"If you finish up what you were doing here, I'll come get you when I've done the drinks. Kyle and I can then explain what we need you to do, or rather, try and do."

I smile and nod as I sit back down at my desk while Kevin walks off in the direction of the staff room. I risk a glance towards Kyle, seeing him bent over the desk, a look of pure concentration on his face. Whatever Kevin needs my help with must either be really interesting or really confusing.

Kyle's brows are furrowed, and I can almost see the tension coming off him in waves. When he straightens and swipes the papers off the desk and onto the floor, I know whatever caused that reaction must be worse than what Kevin alluded to. After several moments pacing with his hands on his hips, Kyle gathers the papers from the floor, and I watch as he closes his eyes and takes a deep breath.

When his eyes open again, they connect with mine, and I feel the flush creep to my cheeks at being caught watching him. He gives me a small smile before he starts to spread the papers out again, just as Kevin returns with the drinks, three mugs balanced precariously in his hands.

"Ellie, would you like to come into the office, and I'll go through what we need you to do."

After locking my computer screen, I stand and follow Kevin into his office, closing the door behind me. Kevin puts the three cups on his desk and looks at his brother, who is still spreading out the papers. He then spots one that Kyle missed and bends to pick it up.

"Something happen in here while I was gone?"

"Oh, freak gust of wind, blew the papers everywhere," Kyle responds, being completely serious.

Kevin glances around the office, seeing all windows are closed, and the fan that stands in the corner of the office is switched off.

"Right," he says as he hands his brother the paper from the floor. "Ellie has agreed to help us out. I think a fresh pair of eyes and her organisation and analytical skills will come in handy."

"Kev, what do you think she can she come up with that we've not already considered? No offence, Ellie."

"None taken," I respond automatically, but neither brother hears me.

I watch and listen as the two brothers speak about me as if I'm not in the room. From what I can gather, Kevin wants my help on the project, while Kyle is a little uncertain. I know Kyle is the creative one of the pair, so I can understand him being a little hesitant to accept my help, especially on something he usually excels at.

"Look, Kyle, I get why you're hesitant, but we've not come up with anything useful, and Ellie is as good as anyone else out there. Besides, if she is serious about becoming a designer, she needs to see things like this. A little out of the box thinking can't do any harm, can it?"

I look between the brothers, stopping on Kyle when he looks at me again. Just seeing those green eyes aimed in my direction causes my body to react. I need to find a way to stop that from happening before it gets embarrassing.

"Okay, fine. We'll give the new girl a chance."

"I might be the new girl, but I do have a name you know."

I stop myself from saying anything further and almost slap my hand over my mouth when both men turn to look at me. What did I just say? I didn't mean to say anything, but after hearing Kyle refer to me as the 'new girl' rather than by my name, it just rubbed me up the wrong way, and I just reacted.

"I'm sorry. I didn't mean—"

"No. Ellie, you were right to call me out," Kyle says as he takes a step away from the desk and stuffs his hands into his pockets. "I'm sorry. I shall be more considerate in the future."

"Thank you," I reply, more than a little surprised that he apologised, but it did appear to be sincere. "What exactly is it you want me to try and help with?"

I pick up my mug from the desk and take a sip of the contents as Kevin and Kyle put the paperwork in some order. When they step back, I move forward and take a look at the papers in front of me. I can feel the eyes of both brothers on me and try and ignore the pressure I feel to help them.

"The dimensions don't add up. This wall here should be at least one metre longer, according to the blueprints." I point out what I mean, and both brothers nod.

"Exactly," Kyle says as he comes around the desk to stand next to me.

As he gets nearer, I resist the urge to move away from him. He is wearing the same aftershave he was wearing on Friday, the same scent that didn't begin to dissipate in my living room until yesterday. *Keep it together, Ellie. Whatever you do, do not sniff him.*

"It appears the client made a few 'mistakes' with the measurements," Kyle informs me.

"A few inches could be called a mistake," I say as I carry on looking at the images in front of me, trying my hardest to ignore the man next to me. "One whole metre is just... well, it's incompetence. Look here, this wall is out by a good half a metre too. You can see that just by looking at the pictures and the measurements supplied; you don't need the blueprints to see that."

I turn my head to see Kyle looking at me, a bright smile on his face. It's the same smile he used on me in the night-club, and it's causing me to have the same reaction, yet again.

"You know what you're talking about, Ellie. I have to say, it surprises me that you know so much in such a short space of time."

Knowing I have to keep it all about the job, I move away slightly, giving myself room to breathe.

"I helped my parents furnish their house. It was about the only thing they kept me around for. I realised then that I could pick up sizes and dimensions without the need for a measure. My parents insisted I use one, just to be sure, but it always came up the same as what I estimated. It was around that time I knew I wanted to work in interior design."

I stop talking, not quite understanding why I just revealed that piece of information about my family life back in Bristol. I'd spoken about the design work I'd done on my parents' house during my interview, but not the part about them only keeping me around for that reason. Right now, we are all standing in silence, and I begin to feel a little uneasy.

"Is there anything else you need me to do, apart from confirm what you both already know?"

I look at Kyle, whose hands are back in his pockets. He has a half smile on his face. Also, I don't fail to notice that his eyes have darkened by a few shades since

I first entered the office. I tear my eyes from him and look at Kevin, who seems not to have noticed his brother's gaze on me, or my uneasiness around him.

"There is," Kevin says finally. "You see, we have already bought a lot of furniture for this project, which now doesn't fit because the measurements are wrong."

"Weren't the measurements verified before ordering any items?" I ask, my question being met with an eye roll from both brothers.

"They should have been, but for whatever reason they weren't, which is something we shall be discussing with the designer at another time. The problem we have is the client still wants all the furniture to be installed, even though we've told her not all of it will fit."

"She wants a specific corner sofa, with armchairs, and a particular dining table for six people, and no matter how we try to position things, we just can't get them to fit, and she isn't budging. This is what she wants, and she's an important client, so we need some out of the box thinking. That is where you come in."

I look between them again, seeing they are now both smiling at me. I start to feel very self-conscious at having all their attention on me, and I need this meeting to be over sooner rather than later. I've got the gist of what they want from me. I don't need them to tell me again. All I need to do is figure out a way to fit a tonne of furniture into a room where there isn't enough room for said furniture.

"Well, I can have a look at it, but it's like you said earlier," I say, looking at Kyle. "What makes you think I can come up with something that the both of you haven't already thought of? That said, I'm always up for a challenge, so if you send over all the information you have, I'll make it my priority to try and come up with something feasible that the client will be happy with. Am I okay to call the client so that I can find out exactly why she has her heart set on this particular layout, and to discuss options?"

"That won't be a problem, Ellie. I shall include all the client's details in the pack I'll send over to you shortly. Thank you, Ellie. If you can sort this one out, we shall both be forever in your debt. Now, if you will both excuse me, I have a conference call with a client, and if I miss it, there will be hell to pay."

With those final words, Kevin leaves the office, leaving me alone with Kyle. I can feel the tension in the air already, and I know I have to get out of here and back to the relative safety of my desk so I can get on with the work they are paying me to do.

"I should get back to my desk. I'll await the email with all the details."

I reach out to grab the door handle but stop when I feel a strong hand on my shoulder, halting any further movement.

"Ellie, can I speak to you. Just for a moment, I promise."

I close my eyes briefly and take a deep breath before turning to face him. As silly as it sounds, I keep my hand on the door so I can escape if I need to. It isn't like Kyle scares me, not in a bad way anyway, but I am scared about how being this close to him makes me feel.

"I just want to apologise for the other night. It wasn't right of me to come round to your home in the middle of the night like that. I know it made you feel uneasy, and that's the last thing I wanted to do."

I know I should just accept his apology and get out of there, but something is stopping me, and I hate that I need to know the answer to one question.

"What did you really want, Kyle?"

"Honestly? I just wanted to see you again. I can't even begin to explain how big of a shock it was to see you sat at your desk last week. I thought I was imagining it. When I realised it was you, the same girl I..." he pauses as if searching for the right words, "...got physical with the week before, it was like someone sucker punched me."

Yeah, tell me about it, I think to myself, wondering where, exactly, he is going with this little confession.

"I was shocked when I saw you too, but we're both adults. There's no reason we can't just move on from what happened and leave it in the past. I want to make a go of working here, Kyle, and I don't want that night to get in the way of that. Let's just forget about it and move on."

I turn back to the door and open it, hoping he will just let me go, but something inside me tells me it's not going to be that easy.

"I don't want to forget it, Ellie. I can't forget it, even if I wanted to."

"Kyle—" I start, but he cuts me off.

"You can't expect me to just forget the night I experienced the best sex I've ever had, and no matter how much you might want to forget it ever happened, that won't happen for me."

I watch him as he walks over and pushes the office door

closed, crowding me against the wood. All he is doing is looking at me, and while he still isn't touching me, I can feel the heat coming from his body. Yeah, there is no way I'm going to forget that night either.

"There. There it is. That pull that drew us together in the club is still there. It wasn't the alcohol or the atmosphere; it was pure attraction. You can't deny it, Ellie. I can tell you can feel it too. Your pupils dilate, and your breathing quickens. We might have thought it was going to be a one-night thing at the time, but neither of us planned on seeing the other again. Did we?"

I take a deep breath and risk lifting my eyes up to his, seeing a thin sliver of green in the dark depths as I feel his gaze burn into me, right through to my core. I know what he means by those words, and he is right. I did what I did that night because I wanted to let loose, and I did it with someone who I thought I would never see again. Someone who would stay a stranger. He would be a secret in my past that I could look back on and smile as I remember just how good he made me feel.

Now he is very much in my present, and anything but a stranger. I know I need to respond to his words, to his question, but I can't trust my voice to be steady in this moment. Instead, I do the only thing I can think to do.

I turn away from him, open the door, and leave him standing there.

15

It has taken me four days, but I have finally managed to find a solution to the problem Kyle and Kevin have been having with their latest project. I've pitched the idea to Kevin, seeing as Kyle hasn't been in the office since our meeting, and Kevin couldn't believe the answer was such a simple one.

"I just called her, woman to woman, and explained that what she wanted wouldn't be possible, unless she spent thousands of her hard-earned money on an extension to her living room. After I pointed that out to her, she was quite adamant she didn't want to spend any more money, and so she came around to my way of thinking."

I'd gone on to explain to that everything she wanted would fit, apart from the corner sofa, but that there was a three-seater sofa from the same range, which would fit beautifully in her large bay window, giving her a stunning view of her new living room, dining room, and the dual aspect window at the opposite end of the room. I sold it to her as best I could, and she bought it, which, considering the brothers had been trying to convince her to do that exact thing for weeks, explained Kevin's surprise.

For a moment, I thought Kevin was going to kiss me when I broke the news to him, and I have a feeling that if Isobel hadn't been in the room, he might have done just that. Now, I'm sat back at my desk, wondering where Kyle is. I hate that I'm thinking it, but I've not been able to stop myself.

After I walked out on him on Monday, he left his office less than half an hour later, and he hasn't been back in so far this week. I know he is probably working away, seeing as he does that more frequently than Kevin on account of him being single and Kevin having a family. I also know that it's stupid and a little arrogant of me to think he isn't at the office, just because of me.

I have thrown myself into work for the last few days, trying to ignore the fact that he isn't here. Each time I look up at his office, I see the blinds closed and the lights off. I haven't been able to stop thinking about the last thing he said to me before I left the office.

It was true, I didn't ever expect to see him again after that night, and I can't deny there is some kind of tension whenever we are in the same room. Sexual tension or awkward tension, I'm not sure, but it is definitely there.

I know if I tell Becky about who Kyle is, she will just tell me to jump him and get it out of my system. The problem is, I have a feeling that if I go there again, it won't leave my system. If anything, I suspect it might make me want him even more.

I sigh and push my keyboard away in frustration before leaning back in my chair. One night. It should have just been one night. Why couldn't he have just stayed in Bristol? He was meant to just fuck my brains out and that would have been it. He'd go on his merry way, never to be heard from or seen of again. But no, he had to be my bloody boss.

Checking my watch, I see it's a little after four thirty, and Isobel is beginning to pack up her briefcase for the night. Isobel never expects me to stay after she has gone, so I start saving documents and closing the various applications that I've been using throughout the day in anticipation of her telling me to go home.

I'm supposed to be going around to Liam and Marnie's for dinner this evening, but I'm just not in the mood. Instead, I think I'm going to have a long bath, a glass of wine and snuggle under my duvet with my kindle.

Picking up my phone, I send my apologies in a quick text to Marnie, just as Isobel walks out of her office; briefcase in one hand, and a stack of files held tightly against her chest in the other.

"I'm off now, Ellie. You can get off if you want to. Just a reminder that I've that breakfast meeting at 8am tomorrow, so I'd like you to try and get here for 7am so we can prep for it. Do you see that being a problem?"

I think about it for all of a few seconds before telling Isobel I will see her bright and early at seven, receiving a smile from my boss as she leaves the office. My bath, wine and kindle evening is perfect now. When I have a night like that, it usually results in me being so relaxed that I am fast asleep by nine, which I know will make it easier for me to get up the next morning.

Even so, I still set the alarm on my smart watch for 5:30am and finish shutting down my computer. Less than ten minutes later, I'm pulling out of my parking space and heading in the direction of home.

Remembering that I have very little in the cupboards in the way of food, I detour to the nearest supermarket to stock up on the essentials, including a bottle of wine and some snacks, before heading home.

I love it when I get to finish early, even if only by half an hour. It means I miss the majority of the commuter traffic, and my usual forty-minute journey is often cut to just twenty-five minutes.

With the detour to do my shopping, I find myself pulling up to my driveway just after 5pm, slowing when I see an unfamiliar car already parked there. The drive can easily take two cars, but with the silver BMW parked smack bang in the middle, it leaves me no room to pull up beside or behind it without blocking either the pavement or the road.

After parking in a safe place, I jump out of the car, ready to give whoever owns the BMW a lecture about common courtesy. After I grab my shopping, I lock my car and walk up to the house, stopping when I see the owner of the car sat on my porch, and he is definitely not unfamiliar.

Taking a breath, I continue up the steps, hesitating slightly when he lifts his head and his eyes met mine. This is my house, my territory. I have the upper hand here, not him. I need to stay strong and not let him talk his way inside again. I can't guarantee what will happen if I let him past the front door.

"Kyle, what are you doing here?"

I watch as he stands and shoves his hands in the back pockets of his dark jeans. He's paired the jeans with a simple black t-shirt, and I can't deny how appealing he looks, not to mention, dare I say it, nervous?

"Hey Ellie. Sorry to drop by unannounced. I need to talk to you, but if you want me to go, I will. No arguments. I understand why you wouldn't want me here."

Damn it, he's being nice. Why is he being so nice? He had been a lot easier to get rid of when he came round the other night after he had a few drinks. Obnoxious, slightly drunk Kyle I can deal with, but nice, sweet Kyle, the Kyle he's being right now, is a lot harder to dismiss.

As I look at him, I sigh. I know I won't be able to tell him to go, but I can still stop him from entering my home again. If he wants to talk, he will have to do it on the porch.

"Wait here."

I carry on up the few remaining steps and open the front door. Placing my handbag and the shopping bags inside, I close it again and walk over to him, indicating he should follow me as I walk around the side and over to the small table and chairs. I take a seat and wait for him to do the same.

When he does, he sits back and looks out at the sea, one hand resting on his thigh, the other on the table.

"It's really beautiful out here."

He's speaking so quietly that I almost don't hear him.

"It is. I love sitting out here of an evening."

"I can see why," Kyle replies, before he turns to me and gives me a small smile. "I don't think I can do this, Ellie."

I look at him as he speaks, a little unsure of what he is referring to, so instead of answering, I decide to wait until he continues. When he doesn't say anything else for several minutes, I'm about to speak, but pause when he stands suddenly and walks over to the railing, resting his hands on the wood as he stares out.

"I can't stop thinking about you, Ellie, and it scares me," Kyle says, keeping his back to me as he speaks. "Whenever I see you, all I can think about is how it felt when we were together, how *you* felt, and damn it, I want to feel that way again."

He raises his voice for the last part and spins around, so he is now facing me. I know that he is seeing a surprised expression on my face.

"That's why I've not been in work the last few days," he continues. "I thought that if I couldn't see you, I wouldn't want you, but that proved to be a stupid idea. If anything, it only made we want you more. I don't think I can stay away from you, Ellie, and I know you say that you want us to stay professional, but there's a part of me that believes you don't really want that."

I close my eyes briefly before I stand, and when I open them again, I see that Kyle has moved forward and is now standing directly in front of me. As I lift my eyes to his, I feel him take my hand. I glance down at our joined hands before swallowing the lump that I hate to admit is forming in my throat.

"Look, Kyle—"

"Ellie, are you out here? I just wanted to see if—oh…"

I spin around in the direction of the voice, seeing Marnie standing a few feet away. Her gaze is darting between me and Kyle, then down to our joined hands. I pull my hand free and force a smile as I approach Marnie.

"I'm so sorry, Ellie, I didn't realise you had company, and such good looking company at that."

Marnie says the last part quietly, so only I can hear as I take her arm and lead her around to the front of the house, out of sight of Kyle.

"He's someone from work. What can I do for you, Marnie?"

"What? Oh yeah, sorry. I saw your car and just wanted to check up and see if you were okay after you cancelled tonight because it's so unlike you. However, I can't say I blame you. He's hot!"

So, Marnie has seen my car. That means she must have also seen Kyle's car. Marnie knew I had company, yet she came around anyway. Was it curiosity or nosiness that compelled her to show her face? To interrupt whatever had been going on between Kyle and me?

"I'm fine, Marnie, thank you for checking. I have to be up at half five in the morning, so I'm just going to have a snack and an early night."

I watch as Marnie leans to the side, making no attempt to hide the fact she is trying to look around the side of the house to see Kyle again. Not that I can blame her. The man is very easy on the eyes.

"Okay, if you're sure."

Marnie hesitates slightly before turning and walking back to her house. I stand there for a moment longer, knowing that Kyle is still around there, waiting for me to go back and talk to him. I glance down and look at my hand; a hand that was being held in his only a few minutes ago; a hand that I swear still tingles from where his skin touched mine.

I know I'm being silly, so I take a quick breath before going back to Kyle, seeing he is now resting his forearms on the railing, looking out at the view. I just stand there and watch him, thinking about what he said. Can he really not stop thinking about me? Am I having that much of an effect on him?

I'm not about to lie to myself and say I haven't thought about him and how he made me feel that one night we were together, and like a bolt out of the blue, I decide I'm not going to lie to him either.

"I think about that night too, more often than I care to admit," I say as Kyle turns around at the sound of my voice and leans back against the rail. "And you're right, I'm not one hundred percent sure I *want* to keep it professional between us, but I am sure that I *have* to. I can't be seen as the person who goes around sleeping with her boss. I want to work my way up by my own merit. I want my work to be the reason I move up the ladder, not because I'm getting busy with you."

I watch him raise an eyebrow at my choice of words.

"Getting busy? There's a phrase I've not heard in a while."

He is smiling at me now, the same beaming smile he used on me that night, and damn it, it's causing my body to react in the same way it did then.

"You know what I mean, Kyle. I'm not that girl, and I don't intend to be."

Kyle moves away from the rail and walks over to me.

"Ellie, any progression you make within my company will be because of your own hard work. You've already made Isobel's life so much easier, and don't forget the work you did to help Kevin and I on that project. He called me earlier, singing your praises. You've definitely made an impression on my brother. That client was being so difficult whenever we spoke with her, but you managed to talk her round, and now we don't have to repurpose all that furniture. You're damn good at your job, Ellie. No one would think you got a promotion any other way."

I'm unable to stifle the laugh that passes my lips as I turn from him briefly, before turning back.

"You can't seriously believe that? If it gets out that we're seeing each other, or even that we had a one-night stand, and I get any kind of promotion or recognition for even the slightest thing, there will rumours that the only reason I got it was because I was sleeping with or had slept with the boss. It's pretty naïve of you to believe otherwise, Kyle. People talk, especially in an office as small as yours, and they believe what they want to believe, whether it's true or not. If I'm being completely honest, even I won't know for sure whether I'm getting preferential treatment from you, or if I really have done a good job."

Kyle steps closer still and takes my hands in his again. I stop myself from pulling them away but refuse to close my fingers around his. Hand holding seems like something so innocent, but I know how his touch can make me feel. Even now I can feel my heart picking up its pace.

"Ellie, I can promise you now that anything you receive while in my employ will be because you earned it, not for any other reason."

"You say that, Kyle, and you might really believe it, but if you had to choose between me and another person, two people who had both done something equally as good, you know damn well you would lean towards me, whether it was consciously or not."

I try to pull my hands from his, but he holds them tightly.

"I'm not giving up that easily, Ellie. You've all but admitted you want me as much as I want you, so it's only a matter of time before what happened between us happens again. But for now, I'll just have to settle for this."

Before I can stop him, he is walking me backwards until my back hits the wall, and then his mouth is on mine. I lift my hands up to his chest, preparing to push him away, but when his tongue pushes past my lips and he presses his hips into mine, any reservations I have vanish.

16

$\mathcal{I}$'m not sure what has come over me. Just having her so close and hearing her honest confession about why she is hesitant about us being together, made me want to feel her against me again.

So I kissed her. I am still kissing her now, and she isn't pushing me away. That is only encouraging me to continue as I feel her fingers flex against my chest, bunching in the material of my t-shirt.

She is just as responsive as I remember as she tilts her head, allowing me to deepen the kiss. My hands tighten at her waist as I tug at the material of her top, needing to feel her. When my hands connect with the skin of her stomach, I groan. It's just as soft as I remember, and it takes everything inside me not to move my hands up to her breasts.

When she copies my actions, I jump as I feel her cool hands connect with my stomach. She slowly slides them up and over my chest, before bringing them back down to hook in the belt loops on my jeans. I feel the change in her instantly as she pulls away and breaks the kiss, but she doesn't move from my hold.

"We can't do this, Kyle. I can't work with you and be with you. I want both, but I can't have both, and yes, that sucks, but that's just the way it is."

"Who says you can't have both?"

"I do," she almost shouts. "My job is too important to me. We've talked about this, Kyle."

I feel her free herself from my belt loops and her hands go back up to my chest. This time, she gently pushes me away, and no matter how much I don't want to, I take a step back and watch as Ellie lets her hands fall to her sides as she sighs.

"You need to go, Kyle."

She turns to walk away from me, but I instinctively reach out and take her arm, relieved when she doesn't pull away, but neither does she turn to look at me.

"Go, Kyle. Please."

I can't be sure, but I think I hear her voice break as she reaches up to touch my hand. She briefly links her fingers with mine, before removing my hand from her arm and rushing away. I hear the front door open and close, and I'm left on the porch.

Alone.

I keep my eyes on the spot where she vanished and fight the urge to kick at something, anything, to vent my frustrations. The passion and lust that was coursing through my veins only a few moments ago has been replaced with confusion. Ellie has given me so many conflicting signals, I have no idea where I stand.

First, she is telling me that she wants to be with me but can't let herself actually *be* with me. Then she is kissing me and running her hands over my chest, and now she has pushed me away and told me to go. What the hell am I meant to do now?

I close my eyes briefly before starting off towards my car.

I pause when I go past her window, seeing Ellie lying on her bed, curled up with her knees to her chest. I can tell she is crying, and I hate that I might be the cause of her tears.

I'm torn. Should I go inside and make sure she is okay, or should I just do as she has asked, and leave?

I stand there for what feels like hours, just watching her as she lies curled up on her bed, when in reality it is probably only a few minutes. I try to walk away, to honour her wish for me to leave, but I can't. I know I won't be able to live with myself if I just leave her there.

I force myself to move, to walk around the side of the house and approach the front door. I lift my fist to knock, but I know she won't answer the door if I do. She'll easily figure out it's me on the other side. If I want to make sure she's okay, I need to do something I've never done before, and enter someone's house uninvited.

As I reach out to take the handle, I hope she hasn't locked the door in her haste to get inside. The handle lowers and I push gently, relieved when the door opens easily. I stand on the threshold, just peering inside, still not sure whether I should be doing this. I need to just leave her be and let her cry it out, but when I hear her soft cries, I can't walk away.

I step inside and close the door, not bothering to stop it from slamming shut as I walk towards her bedroom, stopping when I see her standing in the doorway. Her cheeks are damp from her tears, and I feel the tug inside me. It's the same tug I feel whenever I see her, and now is no different.

I expected her to be angry with me for entering her home uninvited, so when she starts to approach me, I expect her to shove me towards the door, maybe even slap me. So when she just wraps her arms around my waist and cries into my chest, I react in the only way I know how. I fold her into my arms and hold her against me.

Her body shakes as she leans into me, and I just let her cry. I'm not sure what else I can do, deciding that I will leave it up to her, once she's calmed down. I don't have to wait long for that to happen, as less than a minute after coming over to me, she is pulling out of my arms.

She wipes away her tears with her hands, and despite her puffy eyes and red cheeks, I still think she is the most beautiful girl I've ever seen. As she stands a few feet away, I take a step closer, watching as she takes a step back.

"I'm sorry, Kyle. I shouldn't have done that."

"No, don't apologise. Never apologise for how you feel. It's me who should be saying sorry to you."

"Why? You did nothing wrong."

"Yes, I did. I came round here after you already told me how you felt, and I pushed you. I never meant to make you cry, Ellie. I feel like a bastard for making you cry."

I risk taking another step forward, relieved when she doesn't step away this time, but the look on her face tells me I'm not going to like what she is about to say.

"I wasn't crying because of what you did, Kyle," Ellie starts, before she sighs deeply and moves over to her sofa to sit down. I hesitate a moment before following and sitting next to her, angling my body so I'm facing her. Several moments pass before she continues. "I was crying because I realised I need to choose, and I don't think I can."

I know my face must show my confusion when she shifts position slightly to face me and continues speaking.

"I'm not going to deny I want to be with you, Kyle. I think that kiss just now confirmed that. But I love my job. I've only been there a short time, and I can't imagine working anywhere else, but I can't work there if you're there, Kyle."

Understanding what she is saying, I reach out and take her hands, resting them on my knee. I watch her glance down to look at them, and feel her fingers tighten around mine ever so slightly before she returns her eyes to mine.

"That can be fixed, Ellie. I work away most of the time anyway, and when I am back in the area, I can work from home. Kev won't mind, in fact he'll probably encourage it so he can get some peace and quiet. You don't have to see me during office hours. I don't want you to have to give up your job because of whatever this is between us."

"No, Kyle, I can't run you out of your own company."

"Well it's either that or you get used to seeing me there." I pull at her hand, causing her to shift forward so our thighs touch. "You should know, Ellie, any resignation you're thinking of handing in won't be accepted." When her eyes widen, I continue. "You're right, you've only been there a short time, but you've already made a huge impact. Isobel has said several times she would be lost without you. You've made her life easier, which in turn, has made ours easier. You've taken everything that has been thrown at you and worked miracles. If me working from home more often is what it takes to keep you at the company, then that is what will happen, and I don't know if you know this, but I'm the boss, so technically I can do whatever I like."

My words get the desired reaction when Ellie smiles at me, and it only encourages me to continue.

"Seriously, Ellie, I will do it, and maybe if I do, you'll consider something?"

"Consider what?"

I'm not sure how she is going to react to my suggestion. In fact, I'm pretty sure that, going by what she has said to me so far, she is going to shoot it down straightaway, but I will never know unless I ask. The idea came to me, literally in the last few minutes while we've been sitting here. I don't even know if it would be practical, but I figure as long as I get to see her, I will make sure it works.

"Well, you told me that you can't be with me and see me in the office as someone will figure out we are seeing each other and assume that's how you got the job. Right?" When she nods, I continue, "How would you feel about only seeing me outside of the office? As I said earlier, I travel for work a lot, and working from home is no hardship. You don't need to see me in the office at all, but maybe we could see each other after work, outside of the office."

Her expression remains the same for several moments before she pulls her hands from mine and stands.

"That wouldn't change anything, Kyle. Even if we only saw each other outside of work, if someone found out, the same assumptions I've already explained would still apply. The only way we can see each other is if I didn't work for you."

"No. No way, Ellie. I'll give up my position before I let you leave." I see the incredulous look she is giving me and give her a half smile. "Okay, maybe that's a little too far, but there has to be another way. Won't you at least try my idea?"

I can tell she is torn; that she doesn't know what she wants to do, what she should do, for the best.

"I don't know, Kyle. Can I have some time? Some time to think about everything?"

Well at least it wasn't a no, I think to myself as I stand and walk over to her, taking her hands for the umpteenth time since I arrived here.

"Of course. I'm in London tomorrow so won't be back in the office until Monday. Do you think that will be enough time?"

When she nods and gives me a small smile, I release the

breath I didn't know I'd been holding. I haven't got an answer from her yet, but the fact that she hasn't completely dismissed me gives me hope, so much so that I pull her into my arms, relaxing when I feel hers wrap around my back.

I hold her for several minutes, neither of us saying anything. I don't want to let her go, but I know I need to go. She's asked for time, and I plan on giving it to her. I release my hold on her and take a step back.

"I should get going, give you the time you need."

I turn to the front door and walk towards it. Placing my hand on the handle, I stop when I hear her call my name. When I turn, I am surprised to see her right behind me, and after only a few seconds, she reaches out and grabs my t-shirt.

My back is against the door as she pushes me, then she pulls me forward, against her. As soon as our lips connect, it's like an explosion going off inside me. My heart is racing and my blood courses through my veins as I reach up and tangle my hands in her hair. I take a step closer, so our bodies are flush, her hands trapped between us.

This is the first time she has initiated a kiss between us, and I plan to take full advantage as I hold her head in place while my mouth plunders hers. She matches my passion as her tongue pushes into my mouth, her fingers flexing against my chest. We stay in the same position for what feels like an age before her hands push me away.

I suck air into my lungs and try to calm my racing pulse as I just look at her. She has a wicked smile on her face, and this time, the redness of her cheeks has nothing to do with crying.

"I just had to do that one more time before you left. You'll have an answer on Monday. I promise."

All I can do is nod at her as she reaches past me and

opens the front door. My heated skin cools instantly due to a blast of cold air from outside. I step out and look at her over my shoulder, seeing her standing in the doorway before she closes the door, leaving me alone again, and more confused than I had been when I got there.

17

I check my watch for what seems like the hundredth time this morning. Becky should have been here over an hour ago. I've tried calling her, but the call goes straight to voicemail. It's unlike Becky not to answer her phone, even when she is driving. The Bluetooth facility in her car means she can do so safely without touching her phone, so why isn't she answering?

Dialling the number again, I almost scream when I hear the familiar voicemail message for what must be the tenth time.

"Becky, where are you? Why aren't you answering your phone? Call me back."

Deciding that staring out of the window isn't going to speed up time, I go over to the sofa and fall down amongst the cushions. I have no idea why I am so anxious about Becky coming to visit. No, that's a lie, I know exactly why I'm anxious.

I have an ulterior motive for inviting Becky down for the weekend. I need to talk to someone about Kyle and what I should do about the situation I'm in. I know that Becky will cut through the bullshit and tell me how it is. I know that the reality of being with Kyle on a more regular basis could be so very different from the fantasy of the one-night stand. I've been with Kyle once, and that one time was mind-blowing, but was that feeling because of how it happened?

We were strangers in a night club sneaking off for a quickie, and it was one hell of a quickie. Had the danger of knowing we could be discovered at any time, and the fact we were doing something so dirty, added to the thrill? If I did give Kyle a chance, would it always be like that, or would the fact that we wouldn't be doing anything that would be considered taboo reduce the excitement?

I promised Kyle I would think about what he proposed last night. It had been all I could think about at work today, and I'm no closer to making a decision. Every time I looked up and saw his empty office, I remembered that if I agree to his request, the office will remain empty for the foreseeable future.

When Isobel told me I could finish at lunchtime as she was leaving early for a long weekend with her partner, I got straight on the phone to Becky and made my own weekend plans.

Becky jumped at the chance to drive down, and as she hadn't been in work, she threw some clothes and toiletries in a bag and set off practically as soon as I called. That was almost five hours ago, and there is still no sign of her.

I'm about to call her again when I hear the rumble of a car engine and the blare of cheesy eighties music. I jump up from my spot on the sofa and run over to the door, throwing it open to see Becky climbing out of her car. I almost squeal as I hurry down towards the car and throw my arms around her.

I hadn't realised how much I've missed Becky since I moved to the south coast, but seeing her right now makes me think about moving back home. It's only a fleeting thought, but it's still a thought I need to address. When I pull away from Becky, I slap her arm.

"Where the hell have you been? You should have been here an hour ago."

"Don't start with me, Ellie. I've had a shitty drive down here, and I need a damn drink."

I watch as Becky stomps around to the boot of the car, opens it, and drags out her gym bag. After she slams the boot shut, just a little too hard, she walks back towards me.

"We going inside or what?"

I fold my arms and don't move, waiting for Becky to continue her strop or at least apologise for being snappy with me. When she sighs, I get what I am waiting for.

"Sorry, Ellie, can we go inside, and I'll fill you in."

I see the look on my friend's face and let my arms fall to my sides, before linking one with Becky's as we move forward and up the few steps that lead to the front door. As soon as we are inside, Becky drops her bag and I make my way to the kitchen, returning a few moments later with two large glasses of wine. As I pass one to Becky, I take a sip of my own and watch as Becky takes in her surroundings.

"This place is stunning, Ellie. You really landed on your feet. Do I have a room, or am I sharing with you like we used to when we were kids?"

It's clear whatever happened on Becky's drive down here is now forgotten, and I let out a small laugh as I remember all the times we slept at each other's houses when we were younger. As we both only had single beds, the other had to sleep on the floor in a sleeping bag, and no matter where we were, it always seemed to be me that got the floor, even in my own damn house, so we usually wound up squeezing into the single bed.

"No, you have your own room. It's over here."

I lead Becky forward until we are standing outside the guest room, and I open the door. I spent over an hour in here earlier, making sure Becky would have everything she needs. Like mine, the room is decorated in lilacs and creams, with linen on the large double bed to match.

The single aspect window looks out over the town below, and the usual bedroom furniture of a wardrobe, chest of drawers and bedside table complete the room. Becky is nodding as she takes a few steps into the room.

"If you ever need a roommate, give me a shout. I think I could be very happy in here."

I roll my eyes, knowing that Becky is only half joking. I have a feeling that if I were to offer Becky the spare room on a more permanent basis, she would jump at the chance. She isn't particularly close to her family, has no one special in her life, and she hates her job with a passion. There is nothing keeping her in Bristol.

As Becky wanders around what will be her room for the next couple of days, I ponder how I am going to bring up the subject of me, Kyle, and his proposition. Should I do it tonight, or wait until later in the weekend?

I'm not sure what Becky is going to say to me when I tell her. Whether she is going to tell me to steer clear of him or jump him every chance I get. Knowing Becky, it will probably be the latter, but I am never going to know unless I say something.

Ninety minutes later, we are on our second bottle of wine and I am feeling as relaxed as I've felt in a long time. Becky has been filling me in on everything that has gone on since I left

Bristol and she's had me reduced to tears of laughter more than once. I still haven't said anything about Kyle but decide that now is as good a time as any.

"Hey Bex, you remember that guy that I..." I pause, wondering how to phrase it.

"You mean the guy you shagged in a nightclub?" When I just stare, Becky continues, "What about him?"

Here goes nothing.

"He's my boss."

I take a big gulp of my wine and look at Becky over the top of my glass. She is just staring at me, her expression unreadable, and for a moment I'm not sure if she heard me, until a huge grin spreads across her face.

"Seriously? How the fuck did that happen?"

I now have her full attention. Becky has tucked her knees underneath her and turned her body, so she is directly in front of me. Her expression is telling me that she wants details.

"Pure coincidence. I was here almost a week before I saw him. I wasn't sure at first, but when he looked at me with those green eyes of his, I almost jumped up and ran out. I mean, what are the odds, Becky?"

"Is he still as hot as he looked in the club?"

I try to look shocked at Becky's question, making my best 'I can't believe you just asked that' face, but fail when I smile.

"Oh yeah, like you wouldn't believe, and want to know what's making things even harder to say no to him? He's a really nice guy too."

I lift my glass to my lips, realising it's empty, so I stand and walk into the kitchen. I open the fridge and grab the bottle of wine we started earlier, jumping when I hear Becky's voice from behind me.

"So, are you going to go there again?"

I don't need to hear Becky say the exact words. I know

exactly what she is referring to, and this is one of the reasons I asked Becky to come visit this weekend. She has just asked me the one question I have been asking myself practically every day since I realised who Kyle was.

Do I *want* to go there again? No question about it, but *should* I go there again? That is the question I need help answering. Kyle has made it abundantly clear he wants to, albeit in secret. If I do decide to do what he has suggested, will I be able to hide how I feel when I'm around him?

He said I won't have to see him in the office, but that is just ridiculous. He owns the company. How is he supposed to run the place if he's never there? There is no way he can guarantee that I will never have to see him while I'm at work, and I know myself well enough to know how I'd react if that were to happen.

"I need to talk to you about that, Bex. I'm so confused," I say as I go to put the bottle back in the fridge.

"Bring the bottle and tell me what's got you so confused about Mr Hotty."

After closing the fridge door, I follow Becky back into the living room and we retake our positions on the sofa.

"Spill it, woman," Becky says as she takes hold of the wine bottle so she can refill her glass. "And don't skip any of the details."

And knowing Becky would know if I did, I tell her everything.

18

*G*od, I hate hangovers.

I have no idea how much we drank last night. We polished off the three bottles of wine I had in my fridge, then Becky retrieved a bottle of vodka from her overnight bag. If the thumping in my head is anything to go by, we drunk a good portion of that too.

Throwing the covers off, I swing my legs around and get out of bed. Crossing the room, I grab my robe from the back of the door and step out into the living room, not surprised to see the door to Becky's room is still closed.

After making coffee, I head out onto the porch and sit at the small table. My mind drifts back to the conversation I had with Becky the night before. As expected, she started off by telling me I should jump Kyle at least one more time before deciding what to do, but when I explained how I felt, Becky softened.

I told her that *wanting* to jump his bones wasn't an issue. It was the possible repercussions that worried me. Becky understood my concerns but also said that I need to do what feels right, and, to use her words, screw the repercussions.

People will think what they believe to be true, and even if I was to scream until I am blue in the face that I got the job on my own merits, some people would still think otherwise, even if a pile of evidence was in front of them. I must admit, when we had eventually gone to bed, I was still confused, and had lain there thinking for at least an hour before sleep had taken over.

I'm still not sure what I'm going to do about Kyle, but I have decided that I'm not going to think about it today. Becky and I have decided to go down to the beach for a few hours, then walk into town for some retail therapy. I told her about the boutique shop that I found, and Becky is just dying to spend some of her money on something cute and flirty, and I want to get those red and black heels I saw last time I was there.

After shopping, we'll come back here to shower and change, and then head out to the cocktail bar that I've gone to so many times with the girls from work. I know Becky will love the place, and it's a new cocktail menu for her to work towards completing.

I take a sip of my coffee and sigh as I look out over the town below. In just a few short weeks, I've come to love it here on the coast. I always thought I was a city girl but have realised how wrong I was. I know I will hate it if my time here comes to an end, if I find myself back in Bristol at a job I hate but need in order to pay my way. That is the last thing I want to happen, and I need to do whatever it takes so that it doesn't.

Turning my head when I hear the patio door open, I smile when I see that Becky looks just as rough as I feel. It gives me a small measure of relief that I'm not the only one feeling the after-effects of the night before. Becky sits next to me on the porch with her hands wrapped around a large mug of coffee, and just looks at me through half open eyes.

"What the fuck did we drink last night?"

"Too much," I say after taking another sip of life-giving coffee. "There's paracetamol in the bathroom cabinet if you need it."

Becky puts her mug on the table and pushes herself out of her chair, saying, "I think I love you," before hurrying back into the house, returning a few moments later with a glass of water. She returns to her seat and puts two tablets in her mouth, before downing the water. She then puts the now empty glass back on the table and retrieves her coffee.

"Did you sleep okay?" I ask as she looks out at the view.

"I slept like the dead once I actually fell asleep. Have you decided what you're going to do about Mr. Hot Boss?"

I shake my head at her nickname, which is only one of several she's come up with since finding out my one-night stand is my boss. They include the most recent, Mr. Hot Boss, as well as Mr. McHotty, Mr. Hot Pants, and the always popular, Mr. Hot Stuff.

"Not yet, but I'm getting there. Anyway, I don't want to talk about him today. We have a day out to get ready for."

I see Becky instantly perk up when I mention our plans, and a smile returns to her face.

"Oh yes, our day out. I'll go get ready," she says as she shoots to her feet, then sits back down just as quickly. "As soon as I've finished my coffee and these paracetamol have kicked in."

I chuckle as we both relax into our seats, coffees in hand, and just look out over the town below. After a few minutes of silence, Becky speaks.

"Ellie, I know you don't want to talk about him, but can I

ask you something?" I shoot her a look, but she continues, "Just one question, then I promise no more for today."

"Go on then," I reply, knowing that she's going to ask it anyway so I might as well agree.

"If you decide to stick to your guns and stay away from him, do you think you'll regret it afterwards?" She pauses for a moment, before starting again when I don't respond. "I know you, Ellie. I have never seen you like this over a guy before. He's got to you. He's worked his way inside your head, as well as your pants, and while I understand why you want to stay away from him, I think if you do, it's going to be a decision you'll regret."

"You finished?" I ask her, hoping the answer is yes.

"I'm finished," Becky says as she gets to her feet. "And now, I'm going to go and get ready. Am I good to use the bathroom first?"

"Go for it, I have an en-suite."

"Oooh look at you. Miss La-De-Dah with her en-suite."

If I had something handy, I'd throw it at her, but as I don't, I settle with giving her the finger before she laughs and heads back into the house. Finishing off my coffee, I follow her, trying my hardest not to think about what Becky just said, because I have a horrible feeling that she just might be right.

"This is the life. You know, I was only half joking when I said that if you were looking for a roommate, to give me a shout. I'd love to have this right on my doorstep."

I grin at Becky as I put my hands into the sand behind me and lean back, letting the sun hit my face. Closing my eyes, I let out a long sigh. It might only be May, but the weather has been lovely for the last week. When Becky agreed to come down, I hoped we would end up on the beach some time during her stay, and I'm so happy we made the time to do it.

Whilst it's warm out, it's not quite bikini weather, so we both decided to go with the strappy top and floaty skirt combo. My skirt falls modestly to my knees, whereas Becky's stops mid-thigh. She's always had legs most women, including me, would kill for, so when she gets the chance, she likes to show them off.

Right now, she's got the hem of her skirt hiked up as far as it will go and still remain decent, taking advantage of the sun as she lies back on her towel, with her arms folded behind her head. She forgot her sunglasses, so she's borrowed a pair of mine that I have to admit look better on her than they do on me.

"We can't stay here all day you know."

"Oh, I don't know, I'm quite comfy right here."

I watch as Becky pushes up onto one elbow and lowers her sunglasses with her free hand. I follow her eyes and see two guys near the water, bodyboards on the sand by their feet. They're both wearing wetsuits, but they're currently open to the waist. Both men clearly work out, and Becky seems to approve as I see her bite her lip.

"Down girl," I say with a laugh as Becky puts the glasses back on and turns to me.

"What? No harm in checking out the merchandise," she replies as she sits up and crosses her legs. "So, what's next for today?"

"Well, I don't know about you, but I'm up for some shopping."

"Oh yeah, I need to get an outfit for tonight."

With those words, Becky starts putting her things into her bag, and I follow suit. When we have everything packed, we fold the towels and add them to our oversized beach bags before walking up to the path that will take us back to the main road.

We originally planned on driving down into the town, but with the weather being as nice as it is, we left my car on the drive and decided to walk. I'm glad we did, as the scenery really is beautiful. Living in a city all my life, I never really appreciated what it was like to live anywhere else. Now that I'm getting a taste of it, it's definitely something I wish I'd done sooner.

It takes us less than ten minutes to reach the town, and as we start walking towards the shops, I check my watch, seeing it's lunchtime.

"Hey Bex, do you want to grab some lunch first before we hit the shops?"

I see Becky stop walking and ponder the question, before responding with, "I could eat."

Nodding at her response, we continue walking, coming to the little diner that I found last time I came into town. When I came here before, I had one of the best burgers I've ever tasted. Seeing as I know how much Becky loves a good burger, this seems the perfect place.

I open the door and we walk inside. We're greeted almost immediately by a young girl in a red uniform. She's wearing her blond hair in a high ponytail, and her face is free of makeup, bar a little mascara on her lashes. She's cute, in a girl next door kind of way, and I can imagine she gets a lot of tips from the male customers.

"Here's your table, ladies. I'll leave you with a couple of menus and I'll be back to take your order in five. In the mean-time, can I get you something to drink?"

"I'll just get a lemonade, please," I say, and Becky asks for a coke as she picks up her menu.

Jotting our drinks down on her pad, she smiles and then

turns, her ponytail swinging as she practically bounces towards the counter to put our order into the computer. I was right about the male customers as several heads turn in her direction as she passes. I smile and shake my head as I think all men are suckers for a pretty face, before I start looking at the menu.

After less than a minute, I put my menu down, deciding that it was a pointless exercise even looking. I already decided I would be having the same as I had last time I was here as soon as we walked through the door. It takes another few minutes for Becky to put her menu down, and she times it perfectly as the waitress returns with our drinks.

"There you go, ladies. Are you ready to order?"

"Yes please," Becky says enthusiastically. " I'll take the double cheese and bacon burger please. Could I get that with spicy wedges instead of fries, with a side of onion rings please?"

"A girl who likes her food," the waitress says with a smile, before turning to me. "And for you?"

"Well, I was going to have the BBQ burger, but that sounds great, so I'll take the same please."

"Two girls who like their food," she says with a small laugh. "Be still my heart."

We all laugh as she confirms our order back to us, and once we agree she's got it right, she heads off back to the counter to key it into the computer. The same men giving her the once over causes me to tut slightly louder than I wanted.

"What was that for?" Becky asks me.

"I swear, some guys think girls are just there for them to ogle."

"Oh yeah, some guys, eh?" she says, and I don't miss the eye roll or sarcasm in her tone. "Besides, they're onto a loser with the waitress."

"How come? She's cute."

"She is, and you'd have more of a shot with her than any of those guys." When I just look at her, Becky continues. "She's gay, Ellie, as in, she's into women. Did you not see the way she was looking at you?"

My eyebrows shoot up, and I just look at Becky before turning to see the waitress is chatting with one of her colleagues, but her eyes are on me. She gives me a smile before I turn back round.

"How did I not see that?"

Becky just shrugs as she takes a straw from the container on the table and drops it into her glass. She peers at me as she wraps her lips around the tip of the straw and hollows her cheeks as she sucks. I close my eyes and shake my head as she bursts out laughing.

"You've got a filthy mind, Ellie," Becky says in between laughter.

"Me? You're the one that's mimicking giving a blow job." I say the last two words quietly so no one can overhear us.

"I'm just having a drink. You must be imagining things."

I just look at her, before we both start laughing. I've missed this. Missed Becky. Whilst it's true that I've made some great friends since I've moved down here, none of them can compare to Becky. She will always be my main girl. We're different in so many ways, but alike in all the ways that matter. She gets me, and I get her. It's why we make such a good team.

We sit and chat about our plans for later that evening, and the waitress returns after ten minutes with our food. She puts the plates in front of us, and my eyes practically pop out of my head at the amount of food in front of me. I look up at Becky and she's practically salivating and rubbing her hands together.

"Enjoy, ladies."

The waitress smiles at us both before leaving us to our food. I pick up my knife and fork and just look at what's in front of me. Two thick quarter pounder burgers are topped with cheese, two rashers of bacon, a huge onion ring, and so much salad it would made a rabbit happy. It's all piled together between two pieces of a brioche bun. The plate is covered with a mountain of spicy potato wedges, and there's a separate bowl with, from what I can see, at least six more onion rings.

I see Becky is already tucking into her food, and I'm just sat here wondering where the hell I'm meant to begin.

19

"There's no way I'm going to fit into anything tonight. My stomach looks like I'm bloody pregnant!"

"Oh, quit your whinging. You look fine."

"I do not. Look!"

I smooth my top down over my belly and angle myself so Becky can see what I mean. She just takes a look and rolls her eyes.

"You look just as skinny as you always do. Besides, it didn't stop you wolfing down that burger, so it can't bother you that much."

I look at her, then look down at my protruding belly, then back at Becky, hating that she has a point. That was one massive burger, but it was so good. I still can't quite believe I ate it all. So did Becky. I think the waitress was surprised when she came back to see our plates both clear.

"We're here," I say to Becky as we arrive at the shop, and I push the door open.

We both step inside, and my mind is taken off my weight

gain when I see Becky's eyes light up as she rubs her hands together.

"Oh baby, come to momma."

She rushes over to one of the rails and picks out several dresses, one after the other, holding them out in front of her before folding them over her arm, then grabbing another.

"Ellie, you shouldn't have brought me in here. I might go bankrupt. This place is great!"

I grin at her as I spy the red and black shoes I saw previously, and I hope they have them in my size. Walking over to them, I pick up one and take a look at the heel, wincing as I realise these shoes will kill my arches, but they will look fabulous.

"Hey, you came back. How are you?"

Turning, I see Chloe behind the counter smiling at me. Instead of the sunflower dress, she's wearing one that has butterflies all over it, but the style is exactly the same as the one she wore before.

"I'm good, thank you," I say, then glance at Becky, who has at least a dozen items of clothing hanging over her arm and is about to start on the shoes. "And this one, who if she had it her way would buy everything in here, is my friend, Becky."

Becky looks up when she hears her name, but it lasts only a moment before her eyes are focussed on the shoes again. She's in the zone, and no one will bring her out of it until she's bought what she wants and spent a ridiculously large amount on her credit card.

"Don't mind her, she's in her shopping zone. We won't get any sense out of her until she's decided what she wants."

"Hey, I'm not going to complain. She can buy everything in here if she wants," she says with a small laugh. "All except for this dress." She vanishes through a door behind the counter and comes back with something red covered in a protective bag. "This came in last week and I thought of you straight away. I was going to call you but don't have your number, but I figured you'd be back in for those shoes sooner or later."

I glance at the shoes in my hand and smile at her, my curiosity getting the better of me.

"So, show me what it is then," I say excitedly, and she begins to remove the covering.

When the plastic has been removed, it reveals a bright red dress that, if I had to guess, will come to my knees. It looks very tight and very low cut, and I highly doubt I could do it justice.

"Oh, I know that look. It'll look great on you. With your figure, and with those heels, you'll look fantastic."

"Whoa, you have to wear that tonight."

I turn and see Becky appears to have come back to reality as she eyes up the dress being shown to me. As well as the clothes hanging over her arm, she has two pairs of shoes dangling from her fingers.

"Come on, we need to try stuff on," she says to me before turning to Chloe. "Do you have a changing room big enough for the both of us?"

"Follow me, ladies."

Within a few moments, Becky and I are ensconced in the same changing room I found myself in the last time I was here, only we have twice the amount of clothes. Well, Becky does.

"Becky, you can't afford all this," I say as I wave my hand around the room.

"Oh, I know, but I'm not going to know what I want to buy unless I try things on."

With those words, Becky begins stripping off her clothes,

and I can't help but recall I said those exact same words to myself before. I told myself I couldn't afford it all, but I bought it anyway as it all looked so good. I have a feeling Becky could be eating those words by the time we're finished.

~

"I can't decide. I have to get it all."

"I told you, Becky. The stuff in this place is just too good to say no to."

"I'm big enough to admit I was wrong," she says as she turns to me, seeing the red dress is still on the hanger. "You need to try that on."

"Oh, I'm not going to get it."

"Why the hell not? You'll look hot, and it'll make your boobs look fab."

"It's just not my style, Bex."

"Well how do you know unless you try it on?"

I look at the dress and chew my lip before looking back at Becky.

"I hate it when you're right."

I stand as I look at the dress again before sighing deeply, and I begin to undress. I know I'm going to regret this. What with my hips and the belly that I'm still convinced makes me look pregnant after that bloody burger, the dress just won't look right on me.

When I'm standing in my underwear, I take the dress from the hanger and lower the zip. Stepping into it, I lift it up my body and wriggle my hips until I can put my arms in.

"Zip me up, will you, Bex."

I breath in as I feel Becky pull the zip up. I was right, the dress is tight, and Becky was right, my boobs do look fab. Although, I can't wear this bra with it. In fact, I don't think I can wear any bra with it. When I feel Becky move her hands away, I turn around to look in the mirror.

"Wow!" Becky says. "Put on the shoes."

After a bit of creative manoeuvring, I slip my feet into the shoes. Before I turn back, I lower the straps of my bra and reach round to undo the clasp before removing it, and then turn to the mirror. Angling my body to the side, I have to admit that my belly isn't as prominent as I convinced myself it would be. I don't think I'll be able to move very far in these heels, but they make my legs look great. All in all, I love it.

"I was right, you look fantastic."

"Let me see."

We hear the voice come from outside the changing room, and we both laugh. Becky reaches for the handle and opens the door. Chloe is standing outside, and she grins widely when she sees me. She then starts clapping her hands and jumping up and down.

"I knew it. I knew that dress was perfect for you. You look amazing."

"Hey baby, you ready to—Wow!"

"See, I told you," Becky whispers in my ear as I turn towards the male voice, unable to keep the surprise from my face.

"Jamie?"

"Ellie?"

I see Chloe looking between me and Jamie, and then the penny drops as I turn to Chloe.

"You're Jamie's Chloe?" I say to her.

"Yes, how do you—Oh my God, how did I not put two and two together when you told me you work at Creativity?"

The three of us look at each other and burst out laughing as Becky just stands by my side, on her phone. We stop after a few moments, and the look on Chloe's face changes, but she quickly masks it and smiles.

"So, ladies, what will it be? Ellie, are you getting the dress and shoes?" Chloe asks us.

"Ellie, if I wasn't completely sure my wife loves me and is secure in our relationship, I wouldn't dream of saying this, but seeing as she does, and she is, I have to say, damn girl, you look hot in that dress. You have to get it."

A little embarrassed at Jamie's words, especially in front of his wife, I just turn to Becky, trying to push some of the attention on to her.

"How about you, Becky? Will you be buying out the shop?"

"Well, as it happens, while you three were having your realisation/laughter fest, I checked my account balance, and it so happens, I might be able to afford it all, depending on how much it costs?"

"Let me have a look what you have, and I'll price it up for you. Ellie, if you go and get changed, I can do yours too. I'll help you with that zip."

I go back into the changing room with Chloe, and she closes the door. Before I can turn and give her my back so she can lower the zip, she grabs my arm.

"Ellie, I don't know how well you know my husband, or even if you talk to him when you're at work, but I'd appreciate it if you didn't say anything about what I told you before, about my history with the Brendan's. I mean, we did nothing wrong, and it was before I even met Jamie, but still, I'd rather he didn't know. He still has to work there."

So that's why her expression changed. She realised that I knew Jamie and remembered what she revealed to me the last time I was here. Now, she's asking me to keep what she said secret, which only makes me wonder exactly what happened between her and one, or both, of the brothers.

"Of course. It's none of my business."

Chloe looks at me for a moment, as if trying to figure out if she believes me or not, before she nods. I turn around, and she unzips the dress, then quickly grabs all the items Becky tried on before vanishing from the changing room and out to the shop floor.

I watch the door for a moment before shaking my head and removing the dress. When I have my own clothes back on, I sit and think about what just happened, and what Chloe said during my last visit.

I hadn't thought much of it at the time, and truth be told, if Chloe hadn't mentioned it right now, I probably wouldn't have remembered how she reacted when we spoke about the brothers. I'd agreed to keep what she'd said secret from Jamie, but now I'm not so sure.

I see her husband every day at work, and Becky has always told me I'm a terrible liar. Having said that, I seriously doubt Jamie is going to come out and ask me how Chloe gets along with the Brendan brothers, but then again, if he did, what exactly would I tell him?

I chew the inside of my cheek as I try to decide if I've done the right thing, and the more I think about it, the more I realise I don't actually know anything. All Chloe told me was that she had a history with them many years ago, before she even met Jamie. She didn't reveal any details, so the only thing I know is what my own imagination may conjure up.

No, I'll be fine, I think to myself as I stand up and put the dress back on the hanger, zip it up and grab the shoes. After a quick check of the changing room to make sure Becky and I haven't forgotten anything, I open the door and go back into the shop, seeing Becky entering her PIN into a card machine, with five bags around her feet. She looks at me as I walk over, giving me a smile and a shrug.

"What can I say, she gave me a great deal."

"All I can say is it's a good job that car of yours has a big boot. Bloody hell, Becky, I was only joking when I said you were going to buy out the place."

"Yeah, well, what can I say. Although, I'm going to struggle deciding what to wear tonight."

"The blue one," Chloe says as she gives Becky her receipt, then holds out her hands for me to pass her the dress and shoes. "With the silver and black heels."

"Ohhh, good choice," Becky says with a grin before looking back at me. "I like this woman, but I will need a bag to match the shoes."

I shake my head at her in amusement as she goes back into the store, coming back a few moments later with a small black bag, with a silver design threaded through it in sequins. She passes it over to Chloe, who adds it to my purchases. I know Becky will give me the money later, so I hand over my card as payment. We say our goodbyes to Chloe and Jamie, and before we know it, we're back outside, making our way back to my place.

We make it back after twenty minutes and have plenty of time before we head out for drinks later. Becky gets on her phone and orders us a large pizza to be delivered in a couple of hours, when we're getting ready. I've hung the red dress that I'm still not sure about on the front of my wardrobe, and Becky has done the same with the blue one that Chloe said she should wear tonight.

Her dress is just as fitted as mine, and several inches shorter. The material criss-crosses down her body, giving it a bandage effect, and has a sweetheart neckline that, with the right bra, will make her average-sized boobs look two sizes bigger. I can see why she bought it, and why Chloe recommended it. The dress will look great on her.

Now, as I stand in my bedroom looking at the dress I'm meant to be wearing in a few hours time, I need to convince myself of what everyone else seems to think: I look good in the dress, and I need to wear it tonight. Everyone is convinced I can pull it off, everyone but me.

20

"*H*ey Caz, how're you doing?"

"I'm good thanks, Kyle. How've you been? Up to no good I bet."

I kiss my sister-in-law on the cheek as I walk into her kitchen and feign being wounded by her comment, before I laugh.

"You know me too well, Caz, but no, I've been good. Is he ready?"

I look through into the living room of the house that belongs to my brother, his wife, Caroline, and their twin sons, Jake and Max. Tonight, Kevin and I are going out for the first time in what must be almost a year. I've lost count of the amount of times we've arranged something, only for one of us to cancel for one reason or another.

Tonight, neither of us has a last minute meeting, and we're actually in the same town, so here I am, waiting for my brother to shift his ass so that we can go out for a massive steak and several rounds of drinks.

"He's just finishing up a call with a client," she says, and my reaction to that must show on my face, as she continues, "Don't panic, he's just checking on something. He'll be done shortly."

I peer into the living room again and see Kevin come into view. He's got his phone to his ear, which is his usual pose most of the time, and his other hand is waving around wildly as he talks. I know my brother, and I can see the tension across his shoulders. I can't quite make out what he's saying, and I take the fact that he's not raising his voice as a good sign.

His free hand goes to his hip as he turns. Seeing me, he gives me a nod and holds his hand up to indicate he'll be a few minutes. I nod in response and look at Caz, who is busy loading the dishwasher.

"It's very quiet here. Where are the boys?"

"They're at a sleepover at a friend's house just down the street. You just missed them actually. They'll be back for dinner tomorrow. You want to come round? We'll have plenty. I'm sure the boys will love to see you."

I'd love to see the boys too. They turned five only three weeks ago, and I've yet to give them their presents. Work has been crazy, and I've just not had the time to come round. Sure, I could have given them to Kevin to pass to them, but I want to be there when they open them, so if that means they get the gifts after their birthday, so be it.

"I'd love to, thanks, Caz. I can finally give the boys their birthday presents."

"Thank God for that. They've been driving us crazy asking when they will get them," she says with a small laugh. "I don't know why you just don't give them to your brother."

I shrug and start to respond, when Kevin's voice gets louder. I turn to see him walking through to the kitchen. The tension is gone from his shoulders, and he's almost smiling, which is a rarity for my brother. I breathe out when I hear the words that will end the call.

"Yes, that's fine, thanks for your time. Hey bro, you ready to go?"

"Hey, I'm here waiting for you. What was all that about?"

"Oh, just the Walkerson account. I wanted to check that we've received payment. You know what they can be like."

Do I ever. Evelyn and Fred Walkerson have been clients of ours for many years. Their need to completely revamp their home every twelve months has done wonders for our bottom line. But getting money out of them is like getting blood from a stone.

Oh, they always pay up eventually, but it usually happens after me, Kevin, or both of us have made calls to them to remind them their balance is outstanding. We completed their latest revamp three weeks ago, and as of close of business yesterday, the account was still unpaid.

"And are they all paid up now?"

"As of five minutes ago, yes. Anyway, shall we be going? There's a huge steak out there with my name on it."

"After you, brother."

Kevin walks over and gives Caz a kiss before he heads towards the front door. As we stand on the porch, he gets out his phone and sorts out a taxi, which arrives after less than five minutes. Seeing as we're planning on drinking tonight, neither of us wanted to drive.

Ten minutes later, the car pulls up outside Pepper's Steakhouse & Grill. It's the only steakhouse within a twenty-mile radius of town, and it has some of the best steak I've ever tasted. Kevin pays the driver and we both climb out and walk towards the entrance. Within a few minutes we're seated, and each have a bottle of beer in front of us.

One of the good things about being a business owner in the area, and a regular at the only steakhouse in town, is the people know what you like. Kevin and I didn't even order drinks, but after only a few moments, two of our preferred beers arrived at the table.

"So, little brother. What's been going on with you lately? I've hardly seen you round the office the last week or so."

I look at Kevin as I take a swig of my beer before placing it back on the table. If anyone is going to notice my absence from the office, it's going to be him. Whilst it's true I am the one who does most of the travelling for the company, more often than not, I am still in the office two days a week, but since Ellie started, I've been there probably three days in the last few weeks.

"Work, Kev. You know how much we have on at the moment."

"I do, and only one account requires you to be away from the office, and unless I'm mistaken, that account is almost nearing completion. So, what's really going on, Kyle? You've not met someone, have you?" When I don't respond straight-away, he continues, "Damn it, Kyle, you know what happened last time. I don't want your love life affecting the business because you can't get your ass out of bed."

"Whoa, steady there, bro. It's nothing like that, I promise."

I watch Kevin down almost half of his beer, and I can tell by the look on his face he isn't convinced with my denials, or my promise that it is nothing to do with my love life. He's right to doubt it. It is about exactly that, in a roundabout way, but I can't really tell Kevin that the reason why I'm not spending as much time at the office is because I have a permanent hard-on for the new assistant.

I've all but promised Ellie that no one will find out what

happened between us, and that includes my brother. Kevin has been really impressed with her work so far, especially the job she helped us with recently, and I don't want his opinion of her to change.

Ellie is damn good at her job, and she has proved that so many times after only a few short weeks. I don't want my feelings for her to get in the way of her work, and I know that if I tell Kevin about those feelings, things will change. My brother won't do it deliberately, but I know that he will treat her differently and probably not realise he is doing it.

Like a bucket of cold water being thrown over me, realisation hits me square in the face. The way I think my brother will react is exactly what Ellie has been talking about. People's opinions or assumptions about us getting in the way of her career. She said that people will probably judge and not even realise they are doing it, which is exactly what I think would happen with Kevin. She'd been right all along, and in my lust-induced state, I hadn't listened to her.

"Kyle, I don't know what's going on with you, but if you let it affect the company, I swear—"

"Kev, trust me. Everything is good. Nothing will affect the company. You have my word."

I can tell that he still isn't sure, but he appears to let the subject drop when the waitress comes to take our orders. We both have our usual sirloin steak, both medium rare, both with a load of chips and onion rings, and the cracked black pepper sauce this place is famous for.

Two more beers arrive at our table a few moments later, and Kevin thanks the waitress, and then begins talking about the holiday plans he and the family have for the summer. I nod and smile in all the right places, but my mind isn't on the conversation. I can't stop thinking about Ellie, and the huge-ass apology I owe her next time I see her.

~

Well, I did it. I'm wearing the red dress and it's getting more attention than I'm used to, or comfortable with. Becky is lapping it up, flaunting her best assets, which have so far gotten us several free drinks and Becky two phone numbers, that I know of.

It's almost 10pm, and we're both more than a little tipsy from the drinks we've had so far. The pizza we ordered earlier was only half eaten, the rest put in the fridge. Becky insists pizza is the best food for breakfast, something I have always disagreed with, but if it helps to soak up the alcohol and ease the hangover I know I'm going to have in the morning, I'll gladly give it a shot. Speaking of shots.

"Here you go, ladies, from the two gentleman at the bar."

The waitress places four shot glasses on the table, each filled with a different coloured liquid. We both look up and see two guys at the bar, who raise their pints in acknowledgement. Nodding our thanks, Becky turns to me.

"You need to wear that dress more often. We've hardly spent anything all night."

"Me? It's your dress that's causing the attention. That and your legs."

"They do look great, don't they?" Becky says as she extends one long leg before looking back at me. "But not as great as your boobs. I swear they've never looked so good."

"Okay, so it's not the dresses, it's your legs and my boobs?"

"I can drink to that. So, to legs and boobs?"

"To legs and boobs!"

We both shout it out, pick up one of the shots and down them. The liquid burns down my throat and tastes of apples. I feel it go to my head almost immediately, around the same time as I feel the need to pee. I let Becky know where I'm going and slide out of the booth. When I'm sure my feet are steady in my heels, I carefully make my way over to the bathrooms.

After taking care of business, I run a brush through my hair and reapply my lipstick before heading back out. I'm putting my lipstick back in my bag and don't see the person in front of me before I plough right into him, the jolt making me stumble in my heels. The floor is getting closer, before I feel two strong hands grab hold of me and put me back on my feet.

"Whoa there, you okay?"

I brush my hair out of my eyes, wishing I could leave it over my face to hide my embarrassment; embarrassment that increases tenfold when I see who it is that I walked into.

"Yes, I'm fine, thank—Kevin?"

"Ellie? I almost didn't recognise you."

I see his eyes look me up and down, and I'm mortified that my boss is looking at me in the same way other guys have been tonight.

"You look great. Are you here with friends?" he says as he looks around.

"Yes, we've just come out for a few drinks," I say, glancing over at Becky, seeing her chatting with the two guys who sent over the shots. "I should get back to her."

"Stay for a moment and let me get you and your friend a drink. Kyle will be back soon. He's just had to go to the cash machine. I'm sure he'd like to see you."

My eyes widen when Kevin mentions his brother, and as if Kyle heard his name, the door opens and in he walks, all six foot two delicious inches of him, dressed head to toe in black. He hesitates when he sees me, but masks his surprise as he comes over, accepting the beer his brother hands to him.

He's trying his hardest to keep his eyes on my face, but struggles to stop them dropping to my chest, then further down my body. It's only when Kevin speaks that he snaps his eyes up.

"Kyle, look who I bumped into, literally. It's Ellie from work."

"So I see. It's nice to see you again, Ellie. Are you enjoying your evening?"

He's acting as if everything is normal, which is good, but his eyes are telling me, and anyone who cares to look, a whole different story. He's looking at me like a starving man would look at a feast, and I know that in his eyes, I'm as naked as the day I was born.

I need to get out of there. I need to get Becky and leave before I screw everything up and someone, mainly Kevin, picks up on the tension between me and his brother. If Kyle carries on looking at me like that, getting naked with him tonight is a practical certainty

"Yes, I'm having a lovely evening, thank you. I should get back to my friend."

"How about we join you? If you don't mind, of course?"

What the hell is he playing at? He told me he would keep his distance. Give me time to consider his proposal. Somehow, I don't think sitting with me and my friend for a few drinks is keeping his distance.

"Actually, we were planning on leaving shortly, but I hope you both enjoy your evening."

I go to move past Kyle, when I see Kevin turn from the bar. He is holding an ice bucket which contains a bottle of prosecco in one hand, and two glasses in the other. I know he's bought it for Becky and me, and the manners instilled in me by my parents me won't let me leave now, not after he's bought it for us. I can't think of a good enough excuse to not have them join us that won't raise an eyebrow with Kevin, and doesn't that just suck.

"How about that, Kev. Ellie has said we can join her and her friend."

"Really? You sure we won't interrupt your girl talk? I'm married, Ellie; I know what girls talk about when they get together."

Kevin smiles at me, and that does it. There is no way I can say no now.

"No, it's okay. We're sat over here."

I wait for Kyle to step aside so I can move past him, thankful when he gives me enough room to get by without having to touch him. As I approach our table, the two guys Becky was talking to move away, and she sees me coming. She smiles at first, but I see the moment she recognises Kyle. Her smile turns into a grin, and I inwardly pray that Becky doesn't let the cat out of the bag, at least not in front of Kevin.

The booth we're sat in is easily big enough for four, but I'm hoping the guys grab a couple of stools to use. I really don't want to be that close to Kyle right now—well, that's not technically true. I do, but don't trust myself to be that close to him.

I slide in next to Becky as Kevin places the ice bucket and glasses on the table. He goes over to grab two stools, before Becky stops him.

"There's plenty of room here. Those stools are so uncomfortable. Ellie, aren't you going to introduce me to these two handsome guys?"

I glare at Becky, who just gives me her signature innocent look, but I feel her squeeze my hand under the table. I'm not sure what she's playing at, and she'll be receiving a mouthful from me when we get back home, but Kyle wastes no time in sitting down, sliding into the booth so his thigh is pressed firmly against mine. I try and move away from him, but as I'm already practically sat on Becky's lap, I've nowhere to go.

"Becky, this is Kevin and Kyle Brendan. They're my bosses at Creativity."

"Really?" she says, acting like she didn't already know who they were. Well, at least one of them. "Maybe I should apply for a job if I get to look at you two fellas all day. Ellie, why didn't you say they were so good looking?"

I'm going to kill her when we get home, no ifs or buts about it. I can only put it down to the alcohol, as Becky always get mischievous after a few drinks. For instance, a perfectly sober Becky wouldn't have encouraged me to have a one-night stand, and I wouldn't be in this situation now. Mischievous Becky can be trouble, and it looks like she wants to cause some tonight, at my expense.

"You flatter us, Becky," Kyle says, turning his smile to its maximum wattage. "But I must say, you two ladies look particularly stunning tonight."

"Why thank you. Don't you think Ellie's boobs look great in that dress? Those babies have gotten us several free drinks tonight."

"Becky!"

I can't believe she just said that. These are my bosses. Is she trying to get me into trouble? The last thing I want is for any more attention to be drawn to my chest. It's bad enough that they're as noticeable as they are, and there's nothing I can do to cover them, but the last thing I need is for Kevin and Kyle to visibly look at them, like they are right now.

Thankfully, neither man responds to Becky's words, but I feel Kyle's free hand move to rest on my thigh under the table. My breath hitches as he gently squeezes, and I grab for the glass of prosecco that Kevin has just poured for Becky and me, downing it in one go.

When Becky and Kevin start chatting, Kyle moves his hand lower, to the hem of my dress. I grab it under the table and remove it from my thigh, shooting him a glare, a clear warning for him to stop. When he just grins at me, takes a sip of his beer and puts his hand back on my thigh, I find myself wanting to slap him.

He said he would give me space. He said he would give me time to think about his proposal. Before we came out, I was considering telling him I would be prepared to give his way a go, but now, I don't want to even be around him.

"Becky, I'm not feeling too well. Can we go?"

I see the concerned look cross Kevin's face, and the confused one on Becky's, but she masks it well and nods.

"Are you okay, Ellie?" Kevin asks. "Will you both be okay to get home?"

"Yes, thank you, Kevin. We can call a taxi." I grab my bag from the ledge behind me and turn to Kyle. "Excuse me please, Kyle."

Like Becky just did, Kyle masks his expression and gets out of the booth, holding out his hand to help me do the same. After a moment's hesitation, I take it and slide out, as Becky excuses herself to go to the bathroom. I hear Kevin say he is going to do the same, and asks Kyle to get the next round in. Kyle doesn't speak until we're alone.

"Ellie, you look—"

"Don't. Just don't, Kyle. I thought you were giving me space? What happened to allowing me time to think about things? I could probably have dealt with you having a drink with us tonight, but not only did you feel me up, you did it again when I made it clear I wanted you to stop. You know, I was actually considering trying it your way, but right now, after tonight, I don't want to be near you."

"Are you ready?" Becky asks as she comes to stand next to me.

"More than ever," I reply as I link arms with Becky, and we leave the bar.

uck!

Fuck, fuck, fuck, fuck, fuck.

What the fuck was I thinking? Why couldn't I have just done what she asked? Now I've gone and screwed everything up, and she probably won't want anything to do with me, let alone get physical with me.

I retake my seat in the booth the girls have just left, and see Kevin coming back with two beers in his hand.

"Sorry, Kev, I'll get the next ones."

"Screw that, Kyle. What have you done now?"

"What do you mean?"

"Don't play dumb, little brother. I saw the look Ellie gave you earlier, and that conversation you were having before she left with her friend. I know when a woman is pissed, Kyle. Before that, you could practically cut the tension with a knife. Please tell me you've not tried anything with her?" When I don't answer straight away, Kevin slams his bottle down on the table. "Damn it, Kyle, why can't you keep it in your pants for once in your God damn life."

"Will you calm down and let me explain?" I say to Kevin.

I can see he is close to completely losing it with me, and with good reason. I'm not ashamed to admit, I like women. If a woman is attracted to me and is open to it, I will take her in any way she is willing to try. That part of my lifestyle Kevin can deal with, but when it comes to me getting involved with people we employ, something I have been guilty of once before, that's when he has a problem with it.

Although, he isn't completely innocent himself when it comes to women we work with, but I'll let that one slide, seeing as it was one time and it was while the office was briefly closed for a refurb, so it didn't technically happen at work.

I know what I'm about to do goes against everything Ellie wanted, but I owe Kevin the truth. If I don't tell him, he's probably going to jump to all sorts of conclusions, and most of them will probably be wrong.

"Ellie and I have been together, " I begin, holding my hand up when Kevin goes to interrupt. "But it was before I knew who she was. It happened the weekend before she started working for us. I was in Bristol, working on the Weston account, and I took them out for the evening. I saw Ellie in a nightclub, and we got together. I swear, brother, I didn't know who she was until I got back to the office a week later."

"And since you've known who she was, has anything happened, because I know you, Kyle, and Ellie wouldn't have reacted like that tonight just because you had a quickie almost a month ago."

Damn my brother for being so perceptive.

"We've kissed, but that's it. Nothing more, I promise."

I see Kevin take a deep breath, before picking up his beer and draining it of its contents. I can tell that he's still pissed, but he's taking the time to think about what I've said, before he responds. To give him a few more minutes, I stand and move to the bar, ordering two more beers, thinking that tonight couldn't have gone any worse.

It started out as such a good night too. I was finally spending some time with my brother. We enjoyed a great steak, chatted about sports and Kev's family, then I'd gone along with his suggestion that we come to this bar, which is when it all started going to shit.

Having said that, I think I would have been able to handle seeing Ellie tonight, if she'd been wearing anything other than that red dress. It was so tight it looked like it had been painted onto her body. As soon as I set eyes on her, the blood helping my brain to function immediately went south. That's the only reason I can give for why I acted like a complete jerk. Now, I can only hope Ellie puts tonight down to alcohol consumption and still considers my proposition.

When the bartender gives me the drinks, I pay and return to the table. Kevin just looks at me, and I can tell he's calmed down, if only a little.

"I'm not losing her, Kyle. She's one of the best trainees we've ever had by a mile. She's got so much potential it's scary, and she already knows her stuff, even after only a few weeks. You need to find a way to work with her, without all the tension and shit getting in the way." Kevin takes hold of his beer and leans forward. "Is she the reason you've hardly been in the office lately?"

I nod at his question, and watch him sit back again, his fingers peeling the label off the beer bottle as he waits for me to speak.

"I thought if I didn't see her, I wouldn't think about her, and if I didn't think about her, I wouldn't want her, but that didn't work."

"What are you saying, Kyle. Are you in love with her?"

My first instinct is usually to shout, 'hell no' whenever the dreaded 'L' word is mentioned, but there is something stopping me when it comes to Ellie.

"Honestly, Kev, I don't know. All I know is that out of all the girls I've been with, none of them, not one, has affected me like Ellie does. I mean, the shock of seeing her sat at her desk the first day I saw her should have been enough to make me leave her alone, but it did the opposite." I pause for a moment and sigh, not sure whether I should be saying this to him, but he's my brother, and right now, he's the only one I can talk to. "I can't stop thinking about her, Kev. That girl has somehow got under my skin so badly that when I'm not with her, I'm wishing I was. You remember how you were when you first started seeing Caz, and she went on that holiday with her friends and you couldn't see her for two weeks, and what you were like when she got back?" When Kevin nods, I continue, "Well I'm like that after only a couple of days."

Kevin sits forward again, but this time I can tell that any anger he felt earlier has gone, and he is now back to the easy-going brother everyone loves so much.

"Kyle, you know you can't carry on seeing her, right? Not when she works for us. Hell, you even put a rule in place to prevent inter-office dating."

"Don't remind me," I say with a small smile.

"Seriously, Kyle, if people were to find out about you two, her career would effectively be over."

"She said the same thing, but I can't not be with her, Kev. I have never in my life met anyone like her. I'm not just going to sit back and let her get away, just because she happens to work for us."

"So, what do you plan on doing about it?"

"I made her a proposition on Thursday. Long story short, I asked her if she wanted to keep seeing me outside of work.

No one in work needs to find out about us, and I will work away from the office as much as I can to make things easier on her. Though I think after tonight, I screwed it up. I'll be lucky if she even wants to look at me, let alone spend any time with me."

"I don't want to know what you did tonight that pissed her off so much, but really, Kyle, you can't be so naïve as to believe you can carry on seeing her without anyone at work finding out? It can't work."

"It has to, Kev. I have to make it work because I'm not letting her get away. She's too important."

And in those few words, I finally admit to myself that for the first time in my life, I might just be falling in love.

22

"Slow down, will you. What's the problem? Why are you so pissed at me?"

I hear Becky whinging behind me, but it doesn't slow me down. I leave her to pay the taxi driver as I practically run up the driveway, hopping on one foot, then the other as I remove my shoes. When I reach the door, I push the key in to open it, and go inside. I hear Becky behind me as she closes the door, and when she starts to speak again, I whirl around to face her.

"Why am I pissed at you? Seriously, Becky, if you have to ask that question then maybe you're not as good of a friend as I thought you were. I told you everything that happened between Kyle and me. I told you I needed time to think about what he asked me, yet you actively encouraged them to sit in the booth with us. You blatantly drew attention to me and what I'm wearing, knowing damn well what went on between Kyle and I, and how uncomfortable I felt in this damn dress."

I pause to take a breath, not giving Becky the chance to respond. I'm on a roll now and need to get this out.

"Even if nothing had happened between us, I have to work with them, Becky. Was it your intention to embarrass me tonight? As soon as you realised who they were, did you formulate a plan in that brain of yours to mortify me so that I wouldn't be able to go back into work and look them in the face. You know, it wouldn't surprise me if that was your plan all along. Anything to get me back to Bristol, right? You've hated the fact I moved away from the moment I told you."

"Now you just wait right there, Ellie. Yes, I hate that you moved away. I still hate that you're down here and I'm stuck up there, but that's only because I'm jealous that you got out and I can't, so don't you dare accuse me of trying to sabotage your job here."

She's pissed, but so am I. We're both bordering on being drunk, and there is no way that this discussion can end well, but she's not finished yet.

"With regards to Kyle, well, you need to make a fucking decision about him and stop blaming me for what happened tonight. Okay, I could have handled it better, I'll admit, but I'm not the one who invited them to drink with us."

"Neither am I!" I shout. "Kyle invited himself. I tried to get out of it, but then Kevin bought us that bottle of prosecco, so it was either say yes or look like a complete bitch by saying no after he spent £40 on a bottle of fizz."

I'm running out of steam, and quickly, as I fall onto the sofa, deflated.

"I dread to think what they think of me after tonight. I'll probably go into work on Monday to find all my stuff neatly packed up in a box and a note telling me I'm fired."

"That won't happen," Becky says as she comes to sit next to me. "You're too good at your job. Besides, I'm sure you're not the first person to have a few drinks and embarrass themselves in front of their boss, and you definitely won't be the last."

I know she's right, and if it had been any other bosses, I'd probably be laughing about it. Sure, I'd still be embarrassed, but I wouldn't be worried about my job.

"Jesus, Becky, of all the things you could have said, why did you have to talk about my boobs?"

"Oh, like they hadn't noticed them already," Becky says as she deliberately looks at my chest. "Look at them. Those are some epic boobs."

I look down at my chest, then back at Becky.

"They do look pretty great, don't they?"

We both burst out laughing, and the anger we felt towards each other is gone as we lean back on the sofa. My head falls onto Becky's shoulder as the laughter subsides, and we just sit there.

"Why can't I get him out of my head, Becky? I've been trying so hard to convince myself that I can't do anything with him because it could damage my career, and I could lose my job, but the truth is, that's all a load of crap." I stop talking and just stare out the window at the night sky, not quite believing what I'm about to say. "I'm terrified, Becky."

"Terrified of what? Of Kyle?"

"No, not *of* him, of what I feel for him." I stay silent for a moment, letting what I've just said sink in. "How can I have feelings for him? We were only together one time."

"Sometimes that's all it takes," Becky says as she takes my hand and holds it in hers. "Ellie, when I first saw you two standing together in that club, it was like an explosion had gone off. The amount of heat you two were generating was something else. You could practically see the sparks flying between you. Don't tell me you didn't feel it too."

I did. I can't deny it. As soon as Becky pointed out he was watching me, and I turned to look at him, I felt it. It was the same thing that had drawn me towards him. The chemistry between us was undeniable, which is one of the reasons I'm terrified of how I'm feeling right now.

"What if I can't keep how I feel to myself, Becky? I feel such a strong connection to him that I know if I agree to see him like he's asked, I won't be able to hide it. You keep telling me I'm a terrible liar. How am I meant to keep the fact that I'm having amazing sex with one of my bosses a secret?"

"You will, and you want to know why? Because you have to. You might be a terrible liar, Ellie, but I still trust you with my secrets because when it matters, you won't tell a soul. You're my best friend, Ellie, and I want to see you happy. I'm sorry if I crossed a line tonight, but what I said stands. You need to make a decision about Kyle."

We just sit there in silence, both of us looking out the window into the night sky. My brain is frazzled, and not because of the alcohol. If anything, I don't feel like I've had a drink at all tonight. The more I think about it, the more I realise that Becky is right. Not only about Kyle, but about everything she said tonight.

I know some things about her that no one else knows. I've known them for years and haven't told a soul. The reason? Because Becky trusted me with those secrets; trusted me to keep them to myself. And I have, and I will until the day I die.

With this new realisation, I know what I need to do. I've been fooling myself into thinking I've not got a clue what I want, when deep down I know it's all a pile of bullshit. I know exactly what I need; what I want. I want Kyle, pure and simple. Boss be damned. And when I go back into work on Monday, I'm going to make sure he knows how I feel.

23

$\mathcal{I}$ stand in the drive and wave goodbye to Becky, telling myself not to cry. It's stupid that I feel so emotional, but it's been so good seeing her this weekend that I really don't want her to go. We've made a promise that she will come back down in a few weeks, and I've agreed to try and book a couple of days off work so we can spend more time together.

When her car vanishes from sight, I turn and walk back into the house, closing the door. The place seems so empty now that she's gone, and I know that unless I do something, I'm just going to wallow for the rest of the day and probably get blind drunk on the wine that I know is in the fridge after we restocked this morning.

Checking the time, I see that it is two in the afternoon, and I sigh deeply. I've got several hours to kill, and I've no idea what to do. I could do housework, or not. I hate housework, and only do it when it's absolutely necessary. As it is, the place still looks like a show home, even after the fun Becky and I had.

Walking through to my bedroom, I climb onto the bed and

lie back, staring at the ceiling. I smile as I think about the weekend I spent with Becky. We had so much fun—well, apart from the incident last night at the bar, but I suppose something good did come from that, even if I didn't realise it at the time.

Since I came to the realisation that I want to be with Kyle, I've felt… I don't know, lighter might be a good word to describe it. Having to decide what to do about him was weighing heavily on me. I hate having to make decisions, especially ones that can affect others around me.

I've always been an indecisive person. It's one thing about me that drives my brother mad. My brother. That's who I need to speak to. He will tell me the truth. He'll tell me if I'm being stupid about worrying about this thing with Kyle, or if my concerns are genuine.

Even though I've decided and accepted that I want to be with him, there is still the little matter of him being my boss. I've told myself that won't be an issue, but I know deep down it will be if anyone finds out. Eric is usually the voice of reason, so I know I can trust him to tell me how it is.

Reaching out, I check the charge on my phone, seeing it's almost at one hundred percent, which isn't surprising seeing as I plugged it in this morning, having forgotten to do it last night. I find my brother's number and hit the call button, not at all shocked when he answers almost immediately.

"Hey Elle bear, how you doing?"

I smile at his use of my childhood nickname. It's been a while since he last used it, and hearing him say it makes me miss him even more than I already am.

"I'm good, Eric. How are you?"

"I'm good, but clearly you're not. What's up, sis?"

"What makes you think there's anything wrong?"

"Well, it's Sunday afternoon, and you know that's when I

have my 'me' time, so either someone's died or you're so distracted that you forgot. Now, seeing as you're not sobbing down the phone, I'm going with the distracted option, so I say again: what's up, sis?"

I should have known Eric would know something wasn't right. He has always been perceptive, scarily so sometimes, especially when it comes to those he cares about.

"Can't get anything past you, can I?"

"Nope. Spill it, Ellie."

"Well, there's a guy—"

"Please tell me it's not Stuart!" Eric exclaims before I have time to finish my sentence. "You're not thinking about taking him back, are you?"

"No! Good God no. It's not Stuart," I say, unable to keep the shock out of my voice.

"Oh, well that's good. You had me worried there for a moment, sis. So, there's a guy…"

"Yeah, there's a guy, and before I came down here, we kinda had a thing."

"Define 'thing'?" I close my eyes and sigh, something Eric immediately picks up on. "Oh, *that* kind of thing. Continue."

"Well, long story short, it turns out he's my boss, and he's a really nice guy—well, most of the time—and I'm just so confused, Eric. I don't know what to do."

The line goes quiet for several moments, and I know my brother is absorbing the little information I've told him.

"First off, I'll let you get away with the short story for now, but I want details later. Secondly, what's there to be confused about? Do you like him?"

"Yes."

"And does he like you?"

"Yes."

"So, what's the problem?"

I listen to him and I want to tear my hair out. He can be so frustrating at times.

"Did you not hear the part about him being my boss?"

"Yes, I did, but what's that got to do with anything?"

"Are you being for real, Eric?" I say, trying to keep the frustration out of my voice before I continue. "He's my boss. If word gets out that I'm sleeping with the boss, everyone will assume that's how I got the job."

"And is that how you got the job?"

"You know it isn't."

"So, I say again, what's the problem?" When I don't answer straight away, not trusting myself not to snap at him, he carries on. "Ellie, I'm going to use a cliché right now, but it fits the situation. The heart wants what it wants. It's clear you have some feelings for this guy, and it sounds like the only thing stopping you from going after him is the fact that he's your boss. Let me ask you this, what would you do if he was just some regular guy on the street, completely unconnected to your company?" I'm silent again, which causes Eric to laugh. "I thought so. Elle Bear, you've always been overly cautious when it comes to men, not that I'm against that. It doesn't give me any kind of joy thinking about my baby sister having sex."

"Eric!" I exclaim, receiving more laughter from him.

"Thought that would get a response from you," he says with more laughter. "Seriously though, Ellie, if you want my opinion, I think you should go for it."

"But what if—"

"No buts, Ellie. You like him, he likes you. Stop second guessing everything and just enjoy it, and for God's sake have some fun. So what if people find out about you? They'll think what they want to think. You can't do anything about that, but you will know the truth, and that's all that matters. If you want to be with this man, then go be with him, and screw what anyone else thinks."

Is it really that simple? Have I been over thinking this the entire time?

"It really is that simple, Ellie," Eric says, as if reading my mind. "Now, screw long story short. I want the full story, and I want details."

At Eric's words, I burst out laughing, and tell the story of how Ellie met Kyle.

~

It's almost nine by the time I climb into bed.

After I relayed the story of me and Kyle to Eric, he told me to have a long bath, soap, scrub and shave, and deep condition my hair. When I asked him why, he told me because when I go into work tomorrow, I'm going to be telling my boss that I am consenting to, and these were his words, fucking his brains out on a regular basis.

Yes, I know, hearing my own brother say those words to me was more than a little embarrassing, but I have to admit, the man has a point. So once I'd done everything he told me to do, I dived into my wardrobe and pulled out the cherry dress that I bought from Chloe's shop. I also got out the red and black heels. There's no way I'm going to be able to drive in them, so I've put my flats next to the front door, so I don't forget them.

I've already decided that I'm wearing my hair curly, so I've set my alarm for thirty minutes earlier than usual so that I have time to make it perfect. I've sorted out what makeup I'll be wearing, and even decided on a specific perfume.

I have never, and I mean never, gone to this much trouble

for a man, but now that I've finally made the decision to accept Kyle's proposition, I'm all in, and I'm going to show Kyle exactly what he's been missing since that quickie in the nightclub office.

Flicking off the bedside light, I lie in the darkness, and my mind wanders to that night. I can replay exactly what happened, second by second. I remember every inch of lean muscle on his torso. The tattoos that he keeps hidden underneath his work shirts but is happy to show them off when he's not in the office. The way he played my body like a violin until I reached an earth shattering crescendo.

I feel a shudder sweep through my body just thinking about what we did, and the thought that all that could happen again brings a smile to my face as I fall into a dream filled sleep.

24

*A*fter one of the best night's sleep, and some of the most vivid and realistic dreams I've had in a long time, I wake up a hot and sweaty mess. After a quick shower, in which I manage to avoid getting my hair wet, I get myself ready for the day.

As planned, I curl my hair and apply my makeup. The smoky eyes and deep red lipstick aren't what I usually go for, but I want to make an impact today, on one man in particular. Today is the day I'm telling Kyle I am willing to give his proposition a try, and I'm going all out in order to do it.

When I'm happy with my face and hair, I walk over to the wardrobe and just look at the black dress covered in red cherries, then down to the red and black heels. I smile as I imagine the look on Kyle's face when he sees me. He isn't going to know what hit him.

Knowing that today will probably end up with me over at Kyle's place, or him over here, I go to my underwear draw, knowing exactly what I'm going to wear under the dress.

I bought the black, lacy bodysuit several months ago on a whim. I saw it, loved it and bought it, but until now, have never worn it. It's classy yet sexy at the same time, and as I slip it on and look at myself in the mirror, I feel sexy in it.

After a few minutes, I'm dressed and ready to go. I give myself one last once over in the mirror, nodding as I admit to myself that I look hot, causing me to laugh out loud. Walking through to the living room, I check I have everything in my bag before picking up my heels and slipping my feet into the flats I left by the door last night.

When I'm outside, I lock the door, jumping when I hear a wolf whistle from behind me. Turning, I see Liam down by his car, unable to tell if he is just coming back or just going out.

"Wow! Ellie, you look great. Too great for work. What's the occasion?"

I smile at Liam and continue walking to my car, surprised that, for once, I'm not embarrassed that a guy has said I look good. Usually my cheeks flame red, and I don't know what to say. I've no idea where this newfound confidence comes from, but I decide I'm going to embrace it.

"Thanks, Liam. No occasion, just another day at work."

"Well, you look great regardless. Have a good day."

With a parting wave, Liam gets in his car and drives off, and I have to wonder if they've run out of Lizzy's breakfast cereal again to be going out this early, especially when Liam works from home and Marnie works part-time in the afternoons.

Unlocking my car, I place my heels in the passenger side footwell and my bag on the seat before climbing in the driver's side. After adjusting my dress, I set off for work, knowing that in less than an hour, I shall see Kyle, and I can't wait to tell him my decision.

◇

Why am I feeling so nervous? I've been sat in my car for ten minutes just trying to psyche myself up to go in there. It didn't help that just as I was about to get out of the car, I saw Kyle pull in to the car park, and within moments he was striding towards the building. My pulse immediately picked up speed at the sight of him in a black three-piece suit and blood red tie, the colours perfectly matching my dress.

He's inside the building now, probably sat at his desk or in the break room making his morning coffee. It's not quite 8:15, so the place will still be relatively quiet. He might be using the time just to gather his thoughts, knowing that I told him I'd give him his answer today, or he could just be pouring over designs and hasn't given me a second thought.

Whatever he's doing, I'm not going to know unless I pull myself together and get my ass inside. I'm not going to waste this outfit sat in my car. Taking a breath, I remove my ballet flats and put them in passenger side footwell and slip on the heels. Grabbing my bag, I check my makeup one last time before I get out of the car.

I'm inside after only a few seconds, and Jamie gives me a wave and an eyebrow lift when he sees me.

"Is that one of Chloe's?"

"It is. Your wife has great clothes in that shop."

"I'll let her know you said so," he says with a smile. "You look great, by the way."

"Thanks Jamie."

I carry on towards the lifts, not wanting to risk the stairs in these heels. When I'm on the first floor, I approach the main doors, knowing that Kyle is somewhere in that office. Taking a deep breath, I close my eyes briefly and tell myself this is what I want, before opening the door and walking through.

As is usual at this time, the office is almost empty. Two of the designers are already in, huddled behind their computers, oblivious to the fact that anyone else is here. I glance around and see Isobel isn't in yet, and part of me wishes I could get to my desk without walking past Kyle's office, because I know as soon as he sees me, he's going to want his answer, and even though I've made my decision, I'm not sure if I'm ready to tell him just yet.

Squaring my shoulders, I start walking, returning the wave of one of the designers when she spots me. Every step I take is bringing me closer to my desk, and pretty soon, I'm about to walk past the large pane of glass that separates Kyle from the rest of the space.

As I pass, I see him sat at his desk. He's discarded his jacket but still wears the shirt and waistcoat with the red tie. I force myself to keep my eyes forward as I go past, even though all I want to do is stand there and stare at him. The man can do things to my body by just being near me. He makes me want things I shouldn't, at least not at work.

I'm almost to my desk when, in my peripheral vision, I see him look up and stand. I know he's seen me, and as I reach my desk, I hear his office door open, followed by the sound of his footfalls on the carpeted floor. I don't have to see him to know he is standing right behind me. Whenever he's near me, I can feel him.

I put my bag on my desk and continue as if he wasn't there. I don't think I'm ready to see him yet, but when he puts his hands on my waist and spins me around, I have no choice. God, he's breathtakingly handsome, and the way he is looking at me right now kicks my pulse up several notches.

He drops his hands from my waist, and I feel the loss straight away. Now, he's just looking at me, his green eyes sparkling. There's a hint of a smile on his face, along with a curious expression. He inches closer to me, not close enough to touch me, but close enough that I can smell his aftershave. I inwardly groan when I realise it's the same one he wore the last time he came round to my place.

I know I need to say something. We can't just stand here looking at each other, no matter how much a fun past time looking at Kyle is.

"Good morning, Kyle." *There, that's a good start.* "Is there something I can help you with?"

The hint of a smile turns into a full-blown smirk, and I instinctively know what is going through his mind. For the first time, he looks me up and down. He pauses a moment on my cleavage, then moves lower, leaning back a little to peer at my legs before lifting them back to mine. If I didn't know what was running through his mind before, I do now. His eyes have darkened, and the easy-going smirk has gone. His gaze is so intense that I have to clear my throat before I risk speaking.

"You know what I mean, so don't go there," I say, trying to sound strong but knowing there was no heat behind my words, unlike the heat I can feel building in my body.

His expression softens a little, but his gaze is still as intense as he looks at me, before he finally speaks.

"I owe you an apology, Ellie. The way I behaved the other night—"

"Was stupid and arrogant, and you deserved a slap across the face," I finish for him. "But I forgive you."

Yeah, that surprised him. I don't think he was expecting me to let him off that easily, especially with what I said before leaving him in the bar. Truth be told, I hadn't either. I considered letting him suffer for a few hours, but with him right in front of me, looking as delicious as I've ever seen him, I can't do it. In fact, all I want to do right now is grab him by that perfectly fitted waistcoat, pull him to me and kiss him senseless, but I've a feeling that might be frowned upon, especially in the middle of the workplace.

"Well, okay then. Thank you," he says, clearly taken aback.

"You're welcome. Now, was there anything else?"

I know I'm being deliberately obtuse, but I have to admit, watching him struggle to find the words, which is what he's doing right now, is fun. It might be cruel, but even though I've accepted his apology for the other night, I can't resist a little payback.

"Well, um, today is Monday," he says in a slightly hushed voice.

"Really?" I say, deliberately leaning back to check the calendar on my desk. "So it is."

I just look at Kyle, giving him my most innocent look, before he narrows his eyes and folds his arms across his chest.

"Okay, I get it. You're making me wait," he says before taking a step closer. "But don't make me wait too long, Ellie. I'm not a patient man."

A shudder wracks my body as I hear the change in his voice. If it's possible, it's gotten deeper, and there's a distinct gravelly sound that isn't there normally. Breaking eye contact, I glance around us, seeing that no one else has arrived, and we're not in the eyeline of those people that have come in early.

"Oh, what the hell," I say as I reach out, grab his waistcoat and pull him into me, my lips pressing to his. I hear his sharp intake of breath before his hands grab my waist. I release him after only a few seconds and gently push him away, wishing I could hold on to him for longer and do a hell of a lot more than kiss him. "Does that answer your question, Mr Brendan?" When all he does is nod, his chest heaving with his breaths, I smile. "Good. Now, if you'll excuse me, I need to get set up. My boss won't be too happy if I'm caught standing here, um, chatting."

Kyle puts his hands in his pockets and manages to steady his breathing as he grins at me.

"Chatting? Is that what it's called nowadays? I'll have to remember that. Very well, Miss Fox, I'll leave you be. For now."

With those words, he turns and walks back towards his office, giving me a chance to ogle his wonderful backside in those perfectly tailored black trousers. He glances back at me before he goes through the door and laughs when he sees me staring. Normally I'd be mortified at being caught out, but considering I've just planted a kiss on him right in the middle of the office, I just shrug and smile sweetly before sitting at my desk and switching on the computer.

Forcing my eyes away, I adjust the position of my monitor so it's not as easy for me to see him from my desk. Now I actually have to either crane my neck or lean to the side to get a glimpse of him rather than just move my eyes away from the screen. Hopefully it'll mean I'll be able to get some work done, without the distraction of the hotness that is Kyle.

Speaking of Kyle, within minutes of him being back at his computer, my instant messenger flashes to indicate an incoming message. I know it's from him without even opening it, and I know that I shouldn't, as whatever he is saying is probably going to be on my mind for the rest of the day, but I can't resist. I click to accept the message, and it opens on my screen.

KyleB: I want to fuck you so badly right now.

My eyes shoot towards his office and I see him looking at me. How the hell do I respond to that? It's not as if I can just say 'okie doke' and carry on with my day. I know I should just ignore it, close down the message and get on with my work, but when he turns in his chair so I can see him front on, I see his hand is pressed against his crotch, and I just know he's hard behind those perfectly cut trousers.

I tear my eyes away and pin them to my monitor, just staring at the message. My fingers hover over the keyboard as I ponder what to say to him. I smile when a response comes to me, and as I begin to type, I see Isobel walking towards me. Quickly closing the message, I smile at her.

"Morning Isobel. How was your weekend?"

"I was good, thank you, Ellie. How was yours? You had a friend stay over, didn't you?"

"I did. We had a great time. Is there anything you need me to do before your meeting this afternoon?"

"I don't think so but let me check when I get set up and I'll let you know."

Isobel walks into her office, and I look back at my screen. I'd seen the messenger application flashing but had to ignore it while Isobel was there. Why would Kyle carry on messaging me when he could see I was talking to her? After his last message, I'm a little nervous about what he is saying this time, and when I click on it, I see he's sent not one, but four messages.

KyleB: You wouldn't believe how hard I am right now.

KyleB: You look fucking hot in that dress.

KyleB: I'd love to strip it off you and fuck you over my desk.

KyleB: You'd be wearing nothing but those heels.

As I'm reading, and trying my best to control my breathing, another message pops up on the screen.

KyleB: I'm coming over tonight, so be ready.

Screw tonight. After those messages I'm seriously considering letting him have his way with me just as he described right now. It appears the dress and heels have had the desired effect, but they were meant to get Kyle all hot and bothered, not me. How the hell am I meant to concentrate on work with those images in my head?

"Ellie, could I borrow you for a minute please?"

Taking a breath, I make sure to lock my screen, not wanting to risk anyone seeing those messages before I stand and round my desk. I give Kyle a small smile as I glance at him before heading into Isobel's office to do the job I'm being paid to do.

" $\mathcal{H}$ ow was your weekend, Ellie?"

"It was good thanks. A friend came down from home, so it was good to catch up."

I chat with Eliza as we're in the break room, washing up the mugs we've used throughout the day. It's almost time to leave, and to say I'm a little anxious to get out of here is an understatement, especially if Kyle really does come over tonight, like he said he would.

After the messages he sent me this morning, the messenger app stayed quiet for the rest of the day. His eyes had been pretty much glued to my position for most of the morning, only stopping when Kevin arrived around lunchtime, and then they were both locked away in his office for the rest of the day.

At least with not being able to see him, owing to the fact the blinds to Kevin's office were drawn, I was able to get some work done, and it took my mind off the images that Kyle's words had created.

I pick up the tea towel to dry my mug and look up just as Kyle walks in. Thankfully, Eliza's back is to him, and she's standing between us so can't see the look on his face when he sees me.

"What have you got planned for this evening?" Eliza asks me as I pass her the tea towel.

"Oh, I'm not sure yet. I was chatting to my neighbour earlier. She might come round for something to eat."

I'm hoping I put enough emphasis on the word 'chatting' for Kyle to pick up on it, and I know that he has when he smiles and gives me a small nod before leaving the break room.

I say my goodbyes to Eliza and head back to my desk. I can't tell where Kyle has gone as the blinds to his office are now closed, as are Kevin's. I notice that Isobel has gone, and there's a sticky note on my monitor telling me to log off and go home. Unlocking my screen to check I've saved everything, I see another message from Kyle. Opening it up, I read it.

KyleB: Let me have your mobile number. I'll text when I'm on my way over.

Without looking up, I type my number into the reply and hit send, before logging out and shutting down my computer. I'm surprised Kyle doesn't already have my number, seeing as he knows where I live. Unless he does and he's just being polite? When I've gathered everything, I stand and start to leave. I'm almost at the door when I hear a voice call out to me.

"Ellie."

I turn to the sound of the familiar voice and look at him. He is hidden behind the wall to his office, and just his head and shoulders are visible as he leans out.

"Sorry, I know you're on your way out, but could I borrow you for a moment please. I need you to check that I'm understanding your email correctly."

Email? I've not sent him any emails today. Hesitating slightly, I start walking back down and step into Kyle's office when he holds the door open for me. Before I can even say anything, he's crowding me against his desk and his lips are on mine. I've no time to even consider objecting as I drop my bag on the floor and grab handfuls of his hair, letting myself get lost in the kiss.

When I feel Kyle try and push his knee between my legs, I'm suddenly dismayed at the tightness of the dress, something Kyle soon rectifies when his hands reach down to my thighs, bunch the fabric and pull it up around my hips. His thigh is now between mine and it's taking everything inside me not to writhe against him.

I can feel the throbbing between my legs and want nothing more than to feel his hands on me, and when he slides them under my thighs and lifts me onto his desk, I begin to wonder whether what he told me he wants to do to me is about to happen. He breaks the kiss for a moment and smiles at me before he leans in and whispers in my ear.

"I'm not going to fuck you here, Ellie, but I am going to make you come. Fast and hard."

Upon hearing those words, I feel the heat between my legs begin to build as my breath hitches in my throat. He kisses me again, and I feel his hands sliding up my thigh, my body jumping when his fingers stroke over the most sensitive part of me. He pulls my underwear to one side, and I groan as he pushes one finger inside me, this thumb brushing over my clit as he slowly moves his finger.

I wriggle my hips in an attempt to get close to him as his tongue pushes into my mouth, stifling any noise I may make. When he inserts two fingers, he picks up the pace as he moves, his other hand wrapping around me to rest on the small of my back, pulling me further onto his hand.

He breaks the kiss again and looks down to where his fingers are inside me, muttering expletives as he moves his hand faster. I bite my lip to stop from crying out, knowing that there is an office full of people only a few feet from us.

Releasing my hold on him, I put my hands on the desk and lean back, rocking my hips to match his rhythm. I can tell I'm close. I feel the tell-tale signs within my body, and when Kyle removes his fingers and begins rubbing my clit, I almost scream as the pleasure begins to wash over me.

"That's it, Ellie. Fuck, you're beautiful when you come."

As if he can tell I'm about to cry out, he locks his lips over mine as I fall over the edge, my body trembling in his arms as he swallows my cries. He keeps his hands on me, slowly circling my still sensitive clit, sending aftershocks of pleasure through my body. He's still kissing me, and I'm in no hurry for him to stop as I lift my hands and wrap them around his neck, content to stay there for a while longer.

When he breaks the kiss and rests his forehead against mine, I close my eyes and sigh deeply as my heart rate slowly gets back to normal.

"I know we said not at work, but after that kiss this morning, and the way you look in that dress, I couldn't help it. Can I still come over later?"

I hear the uncertainty in his voice, so I open my eyes and look at him. His hands are at my waist and mine are still around his neck. Why was I so against being with him? Even though what just happened, happened at work, being here and holding him feels right. Being *with* him feels right.

"After that, you'd better."

We both smile at each other as he helps me back to my feet and straightens my dress. While I look for a mirror to check my appearance, Kyle grabs a tissue and cleans his fingers, and I feel myself flush as I think about what we just did. At work. In his office.

"What is it with us and offices?"

Kyle chuckles as he tosses the tissue in the bin, and I hunt through my bag for my mirror. I check my face and silently thank God for stay put lipstick. When I have my bag secured on my shoulder, I turn to see Kyle watching me, his hands in his pockets.

"So, I'll see you later?" I ask, already knowing what his answer will be.

"You will," he replies as he walks over and puts his hands on my arms before pulling me in for another pulse racing kiss. "I'll text you when I'm on my way."

All I can do is nod at him, my lips still tingling from his kiss. I turn to the door and take a breath before I open it and step out, hoping that no one can tell just from looking at me what happened in Kyle's office just a short time ago.

26

*I*t's been two hours since I left Kyle, and all I can think about is what we did in his office. So much for only seeing him when we're not at work. We hadn't even made it through one day when our need for one another took over rational thought. Not that I'm complaining, but it has made me realise it's going to be harder to stay away from him than I first thought.

I received a text from Kyle five minutes ago saying he is on his way over. I've changed out of the cherry dress and into a short yellow summer dress. Due to our earlier encounter, I've had to remove the lacy bodysuit I'd intended to wear tonight and replaced it with... nothing.

Just imagining what Kyle will do when he realises I'm not wearing anything underneath the dress is enough to erase any trepidation I might have had about going commando.

Knowing he is on his way right now has put me on edge, so I've opened a bottle of wine and poured two glasses. I'm not even sure if he drinks wine, but seeing as I have no idea what to expect from tonight, I need something to calm my nerves.

Are we just going to go at it as soon as he walks through the door, or will we have a drink and talk before we get down to business? God, just thinking about it in that way makes it sound like we're only doing this for the sex. Granted, it's very good sex, but I think it's more than that. I think we have something more than just great sex.

I pick up my glass to stop myself from fidgeting, just as there is a knock on the door. Knowing he's outside right now kicks my heart rate up a gear, and I find that I'm actually nervous. I mean, it's not like it's our first time, so why am I anxious about what's going to happen tonight?

After taking a gulp of my wine, I walk over to the door and pull it open. My mouth goes dry when I take in his appearance. He's been home before coming here as he's changed into a casual lightweight jumper and dark jeans, and I've come to the conclusion that no matter what he wears, he still looks ridiculously good enough to eat.

"Hey, come on in."

He smiles at me as he comes through the door, and I close it behind him. When I turn, he pulls me to him and presses a kiss to my lips. It's soft and gentle, and unlike any of the kisses we've shared before. Those have been full of lust and passion, this one, to me anyway, feels full of promise.

"You look lovely," he says after releasing me.

"Thank you. You don't look too bad yourself. Would you like a glass of wine?"

"Sure. Why not."

I walk past him to get his glass from the kitchen, and when I come back, he's standing by the window looking out at the view. I walk up and gently touch his back before handing him the glass and picking up my own.

"I could look at this view all day."

"Yeah, it seems to get that response from most people," I say with a smile as I look up at him. "Shall we sit?"

Kyle nods and we both turn and head over to one of the sofas. I put my glass on the coffee table and sit, smoothing my dress down as he comes to sit next to me. After putting his glass next to mine, he turns to face me, his elbow on the back of the sofa, his head resting in his hand.

"You're nervous."

"I'm not," I deny, even though it's clear to anyone who cares to look that it's a blatant lie.

"You are. You're as nervous as a long-tailed cat in a room full of rocking chairs."

I hear his analogy and burst out laughing.

"Where did you get that one from?" I ask him.

"No idea. I heard it on a TV show. Can't for the life of me remember which one though." He pauses for a moment before smiling. "I love it when you laugh," he says as he reaches out and tucks a strand of my hair behind my ear, his hand cupping my cheek as I lean into him. "I'm trying my hardest not to rush things, Ellie, but I'm struggling."

I take a breath and just look at him, realising that right now, I don't want to take things slow. After finally admitting to myself that I want this man, I don't want to wait anymore.

Lifting my hand to cover his, I link our fingers and move his hand from my face. Shifting position, I stand before returning to the sofa, but this time, I'm on my knees facing him. Leaning in, I press my lips to his in a kiss just as soft as the one he gave me by the front door. When I break away, I just smile.

I feel him jump as my hands move to his waist, and I flick open the button on his jeans. His hand comes across to try and stop me, but I just give him a look that has him dropping his hand back to his side as I slowly lower the zip. I smile as I realise I'm not the only one who's gone commando tonight.

After giving him a look, I reach in and pull out his cock, seeing him for the first time. He's already hard, and as I run my fingers over him, I hear him hiss out a breath and see his fingers clench into fists at his sides. Intent on giving him the same amount of pleasure he gave me only a couple of hours ago, I lower my head and wrap my lips around him, holding on when his hips jump off the sofa and a distinct 'fuck' passes his lips.

Spurred on by his reaction, I begin to suck gently as my hands stroke his length. The salty taste of him hits my tongue as I swirl it around the head before I lower my mouth down over him, taking him to the back of my throat. As I move up and over him, I feel one of his hands moving up my thigh, underneath my dress.

I know as soon as he realises I'm wearing no underwear when I hear a 'Jesus Christ' spill from his lips, and before I know what's happening, Kyle has lifted me off him and I'm on my back on the sofa, being pressed into the cushions by six foot two of turned on male.

His hands are either side of my head and he's looking down at me. I can feel his hard length pressing into my belly, and now I've tasted him, I want to again, but right now, I can't move. Well, my bottom half can't move. Lifting my arms, I wrap them round his neck and pull. He resists for just a moment before letting me pull him down to me as I kiss him.

His full weight is on me now, and I'm loving every minute of it. Any nerves I had when he first got here have now gone as I feel his hands move up to the straps of my dress and he drags them down my arms. I have to release him so he can free my arms from the straps, which gives him the opportunity to pull the dress down further, revealing my breasts to his hungry eyes.

"Fuck, if I'd known you have nothing on under that dress, I wouldn't have waited to get you naked."

"Technically, you're naked under yours too, unless you have a vest on under that jumper?"

I raise an eyebrow at him, so he knows it's a question, not a statement. He grins when he realises what I'm asking him and pushes up onto his knees. His erection is still protruding out of his jeans, and I lick my lips, something that causes him to chuckle as he grabs the hem of his jumper and pulls it up and off his body, giving me an unobstructed view of his glorious torso, tattoos and all.

I've never been keen on tattoos and have never had any kind of inclination to get any myself, but by God they look beautiful on Kyle. The intricate tribal design runs from his shoulder down his left arm, stopping just short of his wrist. The design comes down onto his chest and snakes across his pectoral and down along his waist, vanishing into the waistband of his jeans.

When he stays on his knees but sits back, I take the opportunity to sit also, leaning in to press my lips to his chest. I hear him groan and feel the rumble in his chest as I pepper kisses across his skin, and when I wrap my teeth around one of his nipples and tug gently, he grabs my shoulders and eases me away.

"I need you naked, Ellie. I need to be inside you."

I feel my pulse spike at his words, and I waste no time in lifting my hips so I can move the dress up my body and over my head, tossing it on the floor with his jumper before lying back down. I'm completely naked for him now, and surprisingly, I don't feel at all self-conscious. The way he's looking at me tells me everything I need to know.

"Your turn," I say with a smile, knowing that he will have to stand to remove the jeans, which can only be a good thing for me. I'm sure the view from down here will be phenomenal.

Accepting the challenge, Kyle stands and takes a moment to just look at me laid out before him. He stays still for several moments, just staring, before I pretend to check my watch.

"I'm waiting," I say with a grin, earning one from him too as he puts his hands at his waist and hooks his fingers into the waistband of his jeans. Within seconds he has removed them, and he is stood in front of me gloriously naked. Jesus, the man really is beautiful, and for now at least, he's all mine.

"I'm all yours, handsome."

Whatever possessed me to say those words, I don't know, but it felt right. The way I'm feeling right now, I am his. I can't imagine being with anyone else, and while I know that sounds ridiculous, my heart is screaming at me to allow him into my life, not just as my boss, but as my lover.

I see him swallow when he hears my words, and they seem to spur him into action as he grabs his wallet from his jeans pocket and sheaths himself with a condom. Seconds later, he's lying next to me on the sofa, and I can feel his skin against mine. The feeling is indescribable, and I'm unable to stop the emotions from overwhelming me as I begin to tremble in his arms. He senses the change in me almost instantly, his face showing his concern.

"Hey, what's wrong?"

"Nothing. I'm sorry. I'm being silly."

"No, you're not, and it is something. Tell me."

He's speaking so softly, so gently, that it only makes me feel sillier for acting like this. If it's one thing I believe in, it's honesty, and even though we have yet to define whatever this is between us, I can't lie to him.

"It's just… this, now, you and me. It feels right, and I'm just struggling to get my head around how I can feel so strongly for you when I hardly know you. What I said earlier, I meant it. I am yours."

Kyle listens to my words, and I see him take a deep breath.

"You really mean that, don't you?" he asks, and I'm sure I hear his voice crack, the emotion getting to him too.

"Yes."

That one simple word is enough for Kyle as he leans in and kisses me. It's so sweet and tender that I'm unable to stop a tear sliding down my cheek. He moves closer so I'm pressed against him and lifts one of my legs up and hooks it over his hip.

I feel him pressing against me, and I adjust my position slightly and push my hips forward so that he slips inside me. We both groan at the intimate contact, and my eyes lock with his as he begins to move. This is nothing like it was in the nightclub. That was pure, animalistic fucking. This is different. This has meaning.

I can't look away from him as he rocks his hips against mine, the friction rubbing against my clit, sending what feels like little bolts of electricity through my body. I try and shift position to take him deeper, but he holds me in place by a firm hand on my waist, keeping his movements slow and shallow.

My emotions are dangerously close to the surface right now, and the last thing I want is for him to see me cry. I try and move, but he's not letting me, and when I lift my eyes to his again, I see that his emotions are affecting him too. If I didn't know any better, I'd say he is close to tears himself.

"Don't move, Ellie. I just want to look at you as I make love to you."

He said it. Those two words that completely change our relationship. Friends and acquaintances either fuck or have sex. People in a relationship make love. Is that what we're starting here? A relationship?

I don't get a chance to ponder the thought for too long because Kyle adjusts his position ever so slightly and sinks deeper inside me, his movements picking up speed. The hand that was at my waist moves lower, and he begins to circle my clit. I keep my eyes locked on his as my breathing quickens, and I feel the tell-tale tightening in my belly.

I clench around his length, and his eyes darken as his breath catches. His thrusts are quicker now but still controlled as the throbbing in my clit intensifies under his touch. I know I won't last much longer as my hand snakes around his waist, to his back, and I pull him closer so that I can hold on to him as the pressure builds within me.

My breathing is ragged as he continues to push me higher, his eyes never leaving mine. Our bodies are pressed together so tightly that I can feel his heart racing in his chest as his lips part. I hear the growl pass his lips, and I can tell he is close as the muscles in his body tighten.

Then, as he pinches my clit, I soar up and over, crying out his name as I force my eyes to stay open and on him. Only moments later, he follows me over the edge, my name on his lips as I feel him pulsing inside me.

I burrow into his chest and just hold him as his arm wraps around me. We lie there until our breathing slows, our bodies still connected in the most intimate way possible. To say I'm overwhelmed would be a major understatement. I'm not sure what just happened, but I have never felt so connected to another person as I do right now.

Maybe it was the slow and steady pace, rather than the fast and hard. Or maybe it was the holding each other and eye contact. Hell, it could even be a combination of all of that. But one thing I know for sure is that now I've been with Kyle in this way, I don't care who finds out about us. They can think what they like. Believe what they like. As long and Kyle and I know the truth, that is all that matters.

fter several minutes, I hear Kyle sigh deeply, and I lift my head to look at him. There's a soft smile on his face, and his fingers are drawing lazy circles on the small of my back. My hand rests on his waist, and all I can think to do is smile back at him.

"Are you okay?" he asks as his hand moves from my back to push my hair out of my face.

"More than okay," I reply as I stretch out next to him, entwining my legs with his. "Can we stay here for a while longer?" I say as my head returns to his chest. "You make a very comfy pillow."

I hear the rumble in his chest as he laughs, his hand now resting on my hip.

"We can stay here for as long as you want to," he says, before placing a kiss to my hair. "I'm not going anywhere."

I'm not going anywhere. It's a simple phrase but one that holds so many meanings. I know I'm probably going to regret asking him this, but I do anyway, as I lift my head.

"You're not going anywhere now, or ever?"

He just looks at me for several moments, not saying

anything, until he voices the word I didn't know I needed to hear.

"Ever," he says, before giving me a gentle kiss. "This wasn't just another quickie for me, Ellie. I meant what I said before about not being able to get you out of my head. I'm serious about this. I want to make this work."

This time I don't stop the tears as I smile at him, my hand going up to stroke his lightly stubbled cheek.

"You're sure?"

"One hundred percent," he says, turning his head so he can kiss my palm. "Now, I'm happy for you to use me as a pillow, but can we move to the bedroom? I don't think this sofa is designed for someone my size."

We both laugh as I nod, not realising how uncomfortable he must be lying here. I feel the loss of him as he moves away and slips out of me before he stands and holds out his hand to me. Accepting it, I get to my feet and we both walk across the room towards my bedroom.

Once we're inside, I flick on the bedside light. I climb up onto the bed, and once Kyle has discarded the condom, he joins me under the covers. My usually huge bed now seems a lot smaller with a man of Kyle's size sprawled out on it. He wastes no time pulling me into his arms, and I rest my head on his chest, my hand resting on his stomach.

It's not late, but I feel exhausted, and hungry. I've not eaten since lunchtime, and as if on cue, my stomach growls, causing a chuckle to come from Kyle.

"I think someone's hungry."

"I am, but I'm too tired and too comfy to do anything," I mutter into his chest, quite content to starve, as long as I can stay here in his embrace.

"How about I go get my phone and order pizza?"

I'm not too sure about that plan, as it means he'll have to

move, but I do need to eat. Lifting my head from his chest, I smile.

"Okay then."

I watch as Kyle gets out of bed and walks towards the door, giving me a perfect view of his naked ass as he leaves, followed by a perfect view of his semi hard penis when he comes back in. He has his phone in one hand and his jeans in the other, and I furrow my brow when he puts them on the chaise lounge before climbing back in next to me.

"Unless you want me to answer the door to the pizza guy wearing nothing but a smile, I'll need those later. Now, what would you like on your pizza?"

"Anything but pineapple," I say. "Pineapple does not belong on a pizza."

"On that, we are in complete agreement. How about your standard pepperoni?"

"That works," I say as I stretch my arms above my head and yawn, opening my eyes to see him looking at me. "What?"

"Ellie, as much as I love seeing you naked, unless you want a repeat of what happened out there—and trust me, I'd be more than happy to, though I think both of us need a short time out—you might want to cover up."

I look down, seeing that during my stretch, the covers have fallen to my waist and I'm giving him an unobstructed view of my breasts. Grinning as I get out of bed, I cross to the dresser, well aware of Kyle's eyes on my every move, and pull out an oversized t-shirt. When I slip it on, I turn to Kyle, hands on my hips.

"Better?"

"For now, yes."

Nodding at his approval, I dash over to him, giving him a quick kiss before jumping back onto the bed.

"I like that you kiss me without thinking about it now."

"And I like that you like it," I say with a smile. "It's only been a few days since you were here last, but things have changed so much."

"They have," he says, before continuing. "Are you happy about that?"

"You wouldn't still be here if I wasn't," I reply, just as there is a knock at the door. "That was fast."

Kyle jumps out of the bed and I take a moment to watch him as he pulls on his jeans, zipping them but leaving them unbuttoned. He crosses the room barefoot, and I lean to the side to watch him go. When he vanishes, I take a breath, still a little overwhelmed at how far we've come, especially since the incident in the bar on Saturday night.

"Ellie, it's for you," I hear Kyle shout out to me and wonder who it could be at this time. Getting to my feet, I hurriedly pull on a pair of shorts and walk out to the living room, seeing Kyle standing by the open front door, one hand above his head, on the doorframe, the other on his hip. He's definitely a beautiful sight, so if the person at the door is a woman, I bet she's in a little bit of heaven right about now.

Coming up behind Kyle, I put my hand on his bare back and he turns his head to look at me.

"There you are. Marnie stopped by for a quick word. I'll leave you ladies to it."

With that, Kyle leans down, kisses me softly, then vanishes back into the bedroom. I keep my eyes on him for as long as I can before turning back to Marnie, seeing her fanning herself with her hand.

"Oh. My. God. Ellie, is he yours?"

"Yeah, I guess he is."

I know I told him I was his earlier, but hearing Marnie ask if Kyle is mine makes me smile. For now, he is mine.

"What can I do for you, Marnie?"

"You mean other than tell me where you found him?" Marnie says with a laugh. "I just need to ask a favour. Liam and I have been invited to a party on Saturday night, but our usual babysitter is busy, so we've no one to watch Lizzy. We were wondering if you'd have her for a couple of hours?"

"Sure, that shouldn't be a problem. Let me know when you want me, and I can either come round to yours or you can bring her round here."

"Thank you so much. I'll go now and leave you with that delicious hunk of a man."

We both laugh at her words as she leaves, and I'm about to close the door when I see the pizza delivery guy walking up the drive. He takes our pizza out of his bag and explains it's already been paid for, and after wishing me a good evening, he leaves as quickly as he arrived.

After closing the door, I walk back into the bedroom to see Kyle messing on his phone, stretched out on the bed. His one hand is behind his head, and I still can't get over how good he looks, and how much of an eyeful he just gave Marnie.

"You know, you could have covered up in front of my neighbour."

"If I'd known it was your neighbour, I would have done," he replies, putting his phone down as I walk over with the pizza and place it on the bed between us. "She seems nice, if a little distracted." When I start laughing, he just says, "What?"

"Kyle, you were stood in my doorway, topless and barefoot, with just your jeans on. Did you really expect her to be focussed?"

He just looks at me, the expression on his face telling me he has no clue what I'm talking about. Shaking my head, I climb back onto the bed and open the pizza box. My stomach growls loudly as the smell of melted cheese and pepperoni fills the air.

We spend the next twenty minutes devouring the pizza and chatting about everything and nothing. Kyle gives me little titbits about growing up with Kevin, and I tell him about life as a teenager with a best friend like Becky. By the time the pizza is finished, we've learnt a little bit more about each other, and after I dispose of the pizza box, I grab our wine glasses from the coffee table and bring them back through to the bedroom.

"Can I run something by you, Ellie?" Kyle asks as he adjusts the pillow behind his head and leans back.

"Fire away," I reply, handing him his wine glass as I sit cross-legged next to him.

"Kevin and I were talking about having a party sometime next month. The company has had a great year so far, so we thought it might be a good way to thank the staff for all their hard work. Do you think people would like that?"

"I think they'd love it. What kind of party were you thinking of?"

"Well, we've not made any decision yet, but I'm thinking of hiring a room, maybe a DJ, or even a live band. Either a sit-down meal or a buffet. I like the idea of making it a formal evening, black tie, that kind of thing. What do you think?"

What do I think? I think if there's an opportunity to see Kyle in a tuxedo, I'll be there with bells on. Then again, Kyle in a tuxedo might be too good to resist, and that's exactly what I'll need to do, as there is no way I'll be able to act on how I feel about him, not with everyone from work there.

"I think a formal affair sounds great. Women love any excuse to dress up, and seeing as 75% of your workforce are women, I think it'll be a hit. Will it be work only or will you open it up to partners?"

"Not decided yet, but I shall keep that in mind."

We both take a sip of our wine before Kyle reaches over and takes mine from my hands, placing both glasses on the bedside table next to him.

"Now, we've eaten, we've rested, and you're wearing too many clothes again."

And with those few words and a wide grin from Kyle, I surrender to his touch.

28

"*T*hat's it for the day, Ellie. Are you all set for tomorrow?"

"You bet. I just need to pick up my dress on the way home and I'm good to go."

"Okay, I shall see you tomorrow."

I smile at Isobel as she leaves the office, and I start to pack up. Tomorrow is the big office event that Kyle asked me about almost a month ago. I don't know how he and Kevin managed to pull it together in just four weeks, but they did, and it's all anyone has been able to talk about since it was announced less than a week after Kyle mentioned it to me.

In a short space of time, they've managed to secure a venue—a hotel just outside of town—book a live band, get a caterer to provide a three course meal for everyone, and from what I can gather, have put a huge sum of money behind the bar to cover the drinks.

The only thing they've not paid for are the hotel rooms for those staff that are staying over, which includes me. Kyle booked the rooms for us and has made sure they have a connecting door, so we can see each other without having to leave our rooms. The sneaking around hasn't been easy, but we've made it work so far.

Tonight, I need to go and pick up my dress from Chloe's boutique. As soon as Kyle mentioned he wanted it to be a formal event, I went straight to Chloe and asked her to keep an eye out for a dress. Seeing as she got it spot on with the red one, I figured I could trust her judgement to find one for this event.

My faith was well placed, as just two days later, she called me to say she had seen the perfect dress, and she would order it in for me. When I went to try it on, I fell in love with it, and all I could think about was seeing Kyle's face when he sees me in it for the first time.

That will be the only downer about the evening; not being able to show Kyle any kind of affection. Since he came round the night I accepted his proposition, we've spent as much time together as we can.

Kyle still has to work away several days a week, but if we're both in the area, he either comes to mine or I go to his place. Despite the incident in his office that first day, we've managed to maintain a professional relationship at work, and as far as I know, no one knows anything about us, apart from Kevin that is.

We'd been seeing each other less than a week before Kyle told me Kevin knew about us. I was a little pissed at first, but when Kyle explained how he'd needed someone to talk to after that night in the bar, I understood. I'd talked to Becky, so I couldn't blame Kyle for needing to do the same thing, and Kevin was the logical choice.

Thankfully, Kevin hasn't been treating me any differently, and hasn't mentioned anything about me and Kyle. If I didn't know that he knows about us, I wouldn't be any the wiser.

When I'm all sorted, I close down my computer and go to

leave. Both Kyle and Kevin have been out of the office all day at meetings in London. I've not seen him since Tuesday, and I admit that I've missed him. I won't get to see Kyle until the party tomorrow, and I can't wait.

I know he has his tuxedo all ready. He sent me a picture when he went to try it on, and I swear to God I came in my knickers. Kyle in a three-piece suit has nothing on Kyle in a tuxedo. With that image burned into my brain, I'd gone round to his place that evening and practically jumped him as soon as I walked through the door.

That night was one of our most frantic bouts of lovemaking. We hadn't been able to get enough of each other, and there was evidence of that across my chest a few days later, when little bruises began to appear from where Kyle had used his teeth to work me into a lust-filled frenzy.

I smile as I remember that night, waving my goodbyes to Eliza and the other girls, who all shout that they'll see me tomorrow. When I'm in my car, I roll down the windows and turn on the radio. The sun has been making an appearance for the last few days, and at the moment, my car thermometer is saying it's 22 degrees.

My plan for when I get home is to take a long bath, order a Chinese, open a bottle of wine, and sit out on the porch and enjoy the sunshine—well, what little sunshine there is left of the day.

After picking up my dress from Chloe, along with a new pair of shoes and clutch bag that set me back almost £100, I'm on my way home. One of my favourite songs comes on the radio, and I start singing along. I've got a job I love, my favourite tunes are on the radio, the sun is shining, and I have a great man in my life. A man who I've found I miss when he isn't here and can't get enough of when he is. All in all, life is good.

When I get home, I park on the drive, grab everything I need and get out of the car. I'm almost at my door when I hear Marnie call my name.

"Ellie! I'm glad I caught you. This came for you earlier," she says as she hands me a box. "I need to run. If I don't see you before, have a great night tomorrow. Will your man be there?"

"Yes, he'll be there," I say as she hurries off to her car. "Have a good weekend."

Marnie waves a hand at me as she climbs in her car and drives off. I just look at the package in my hand, juggling everything so I can get the key in the door and open it. Once I'm inside, I walk straight through to my bedroom, hang up the dress, and put the accessories on the chaise lounge.

Keeping hold of the package, I sit on the bed and put the box next to me. Using my keys, I open it up to reveal another box, only this one is white and wrapped in a red ribbon. I pick up the card attached to it, and smile when I read it:

Hope you'll wear this for me tomorrow night.

Yours,

K x

Reading the message again, I can't stop smiling as I put the note on my bed and pull the ribbon off the box. I lift the lid slowly, and I'm met with white silk and lace. I lift the item out of the box, unable to stop my gasp at how beautiful it is. Kyle has bought me an almost sheer white chemise. The lace detailing is exquisite, and I'm sure I've never owned anything so delicate and stunning.

Placing it back in the box as carefully as I can, I retrieve my phone out of my bag and send him a quick text to thank him. Knowing it might be a while before he can respond, I go into the bathroom and turn on the shower.

I won't have time to do what I need to do tomorrow, as

I'm meeting the girls from work for lunch and a few drinks at the hotel before we all go to get ready for the party. I've no idea how long we will be drinking for, so I'm going to shower and wash my hair tonight to give me more time tomorrow.

As I've got nothing else planned for the evening, I decide on a bath over the shower, so I switch one off and the other on. After adding a generous helping of my favourite bubble bath, I go into the kitchen and pour myself a glass of wine, pausing for a moment when I realise wine is fast becoming my best friend. Then I realise this is my first glass all week, so I continue pouring.

When I'm back in the bedroom, I strip out of my clothes and put on a robe as I wait for the bath to fill. The robe is another present from Kyle. It's short, silky and a beautiful baby pink colour. I love it just as much as I love the chemise. At that moment, my phone buzzes to indicate a message, and I snatch it up, seeing it's from Kyle.

I'm glad you like it. So, will you wear it for me?

I send him a reply, telling him I love it and of course I'll wear it for him, and his response comes through within seconds.

And what are you wearing now?

Clearly Kyle is in a playful mood, and I'm guessing Kevin is doing the driving as Kyle didn't mention they were staying over in London. Either that or Kyle is texting me in the middle of a meeting, which he is too professional to do. I tell him I'm just wearing the robe he got me and wait for him to respond.

Oh really? Can I see?

Yup, definitely in a playful mood. Bringing up the camera on my phone, I switch it to front facing and snap a quick selfie, making sure he can see what I'm wearing, as well as the glass of wine in my hand. I check the picture before I send it, knowing he'll approve of the hint of cleavage.

Putting my phone on the bedside table, I go into the en-suite and turn off the water. The room is now filled with the scent of jasmine, and I'm about to slip out of the robe when my phone vibrates again. Deciding I'll respond to this one message before I climb in, I go and get my phone, furrowing my brow at his response.

That's nice, but I didn't want a picture…

If he didn't want to see a picture, then how is he meant to see me? The only way would be if he were here, and he can't be so—

My head shoots up when I hear a knock on the door. I look at my phone, then at the door, then back at my phone. No, it can't be him. He's in London, or at least on his way back from London. Another message comes through, and I read it before tossing the phone onto the bed and rushing to the front door.

Flinging the door open, I grin widely at Kyle, who is standing there smiling back. I don't wait for him to come in, I launch myself at him, pleased when he catches me so I can wrap my legs around his waist. He carries me into the house and kicks the door shut behind him as I hold on to him tightly before pressing my lips to his. It feels like forever since I saw him last, even though it has only been three days.

"God, I've missed you," Kyle says when I break the kiss, and I feel him pull at the belt on the robe so it opens.

"What are you doing back? I didn't think I'd see you until tomorrow."

I'm aware of how breathy my voice sounds, but I don't care. My man is back, and he's carrying me into the bedroom.

"We finished early so I thought I'd surprise you."

As he lies me down on the bed, he makes quick work of

his clothes and kneels in front of me, parting my legs so I am completely open to him.

I keep my eyes on his for as long as I can, but when his mouth connects with my clit and he sucks it into his mouth, my head falls back onto the bed and a strangled groan spills past my lips. When he starts licking me with his tongue, my hands go to his head and tangle in his hair, trying to get him closer.

He knows I'm not able to hold out long when he goes down on me, and as he continues to suck my clit, my grip on his hair tightens as I tug his face away from my body and slide down off the bed, shrugging out of the robe, until I am kneeling on the floor in front of him, taking him in my mouth.

Now it's his turn to grip my hair as I suck and lick his shaft, taking him to the back of my throat over and over until I feel the muscles in his thighs tighten, a clear indicator that he is close to the edge. With one last slow move up his length, I release him and move to straddle his lap. When I feel him at my entrance, I drop down, taking all of him inside my body.

I cry out at the feeling of him inside me after what feels like forever, and I hear the expletives pass his lips as he adjusts our positions, causing him to slip deeper inside me. As I begin to move, Kyle takes my breast in his mouth and gently bites the nipple, giving the other the same treatment as I rock back and forth.

Knowing that both of us are close, Kyle starts rubbing my clit, and the room is filled with the sound of skin on skin, mixed with our groans as we both push each other to the limit.

After a few more seconds, we both cry out as we fall over the edge together, and I fall forward into Kyle's arms as he wraps them around my back and holds me as our breathing returns to normal.

"Well, if that's the welcome I get when I come back, I need to go away more often."

I laugh at his words and lift my head to place a soft kiss on his lips.

"Thank you for the present. It's gorgeous. I love it."

"I'm pleased you like it. I hope I got the right size. I realised as I was buying it that I didn't know what to get."

"I'm sure it'll be perfect, and I would love to wear it for you tomorrow."

"Good. Speaking of tomorrow, is that your dress?"

I follow his eyes to the wardrobe, where I hung the dress earlier, pleased that Chloe put it in a bag that isn't see through. I don't want Kyle to see the dress until I arrive at the party tomorrow.

"It is, and no, you can't see it, not until tomorrow. I want it to be a surprise. Now, I ran a bath earlier. Would you like to join me?"

Kyle tries to pout, but that only makes me laugh as I move to a standing position and hold my hand out for Kyle. I'll never get used to feeling the loss of him from my body after we've made love, and its only when I'm leading him to the bathroom that I realise we used no protection just now.

As soon as I knew Kyle and I being together was going to be a regular thing, I made an appointment at the doctors and starting taking the pill, but still, I've never had sex before without a condom, and while I've got no problem with it, not with Kyle, I don't know if Kyle does. Before we get to the bathroom, I stop and turn to him.

"We didn't use any protection just now. I'm on the pill, I'm clean, and I'm okay with it. How about you?"

"I'm clean too, and perfectly okay with it if you are. Just

being able to feel you, all of you, I can't describe how it felt, but I want to feel it again, every time we make love." I smile at him, move onto my tiptoes and kiss him. When I move away, he is smiling too. "Now, can we get into that bath before it gets cold."

I salute him and turn round, squealing when he swats my backside.

29

"Okay, so what's everyone's dress like? Oh, come on, no one's talking?"

There's six of us sat on two massive sofas in the bar of the hotel where the Creativity in Design summer party is being held. Mel has been trying to finagle information out of us for the last hour about what our dresses look like, but none of us are talking, and she hates it.

"Mel, we have..." I check my watch, "three hours before the party starts. Have a little patience."

"Okay, how about colours? Can we at least tell each other colours?"

We all give Mel that little piece of information, and we discover that we've got a veritable rainbow between us. If nothing else, this party is going to be one of the most colourful ones around here for a long time.

"What time are your partners getting here?"

Each of the girls reel off a time in answer to my question, some as soon as thirty minutes time, others saying their other halves won't be here until after the party has started.

It took a lot of number crunching before Kevin and Kyle decided to open the party up to partners. Everyone bar a few of the staff has a husband, wife or significant other, which has caused the numbers to almost double. Eventually they decided to go for it, and it has gone down well with the staff.

"Ladies, enjoying yourselves I see."

We all look up when we see Jamie walking over to us, pulling a small suitcase in one hand, with a suit bag draped over his arm. I look past him, expecting to see Chloe somewhere behind, but there's no sign of her. When I picked up my dress yesterday, she said she was coming and that she would see me there, so where is she? As if he knows what I'm about to ask him, Jamie speaks first.

"Chloe isn't feeling well, so she decided to stay in and have an early night. The kids are with their grandparents, so it's quiet."

"Oh, that's a shame, I was looking forward to catching up with her. I didn't really get a chance last night."

"She was looking forward to it too, but it can't be helped. Enjoy, ladies, and I shall see you all later at the party."

We all say our goodbyes to Jamie and return to our drinks, but I can't help wondering if Chloe is really ill, or if it has something to do with whatever history she has with Kyle and Kevin. If it happened as far back as she claims, surely everyone would be over it by now.

I go to pick up my drink, when I stop suddenly. I don't need to hear or see him to know he's close. My senses always seem to go into overdrive whenever he's near me, so when I see him coming around the corner, dragging a suitcase and carrying a suit bag, much like Jamie had been, I force myself not to smile like I usually would.

I need to remember that I have to rein it in tonight.

Tonight, he is Kyle Brendan, my boss. Not Kyle Brendan, my… what? Lover? Boyfriend? Whatever he is to me, I can't do all the things I want to do to him whenever I lay my eyes on him. I can't go up and touch him, can't hold his hand, and sure as hell can't kiss him, which is what I want to do right now, and it has only been five hours since I saw him last.

After we shared a bath last night, we climbed into bed, and after another energetic sex session, we fell asleep in each other's arms. This morning, Kyle woke up before me, so he made coffee and breakfast, which we ate on the porch.

He needed to leave just before midday, promising that even though we had to be discreet at the party, there was nothing keeping us apart when it was all over.

At the time, that had been enough for me. Just knowing that I could be with him after the party was over kept me going, and I was confident I would be able to get through the night, but now that I've seen him, I'm not so sure. I can see that he is trying his hardest not to look straight at me, but he is still heading in our direction.

"Ladies," he says as he comes to stand right next to me but addresses us all. "It looks like you're all having fun."

As usual, all the girls go dreamy-eyed at the sight of him. Before, it used to irritate me, now it just amuses me, and I love to tease Kyle whenever it happens. He acts like he's oblivious to it, but I know he sees it every time he walks into the office. His response is always something like he doesn't care that others look at him, the only female attention he wants is from me. Whilst it's more than a little cliché, it still makes me smile when he says it.

Everyone is making small talk with Kyle, when I notice two of the waiters walking over with a bottle in a fancy ice bucket, and another with a tray carrying champagne glasses. I give Kyle a look, only to see him smirking. I know that smirk is intended for me, but he's managing to keep it under wraps, better than I am anyway. When the waiters put the glasses and the ice bucket containing the champagne on the table between us, there is a chorus of 'thank you' from everyone, including me.

"Enjoy, ladies. I shall see you all later."

When he turns to walk away, he briefly smiles down at me and his hand brushes my shoulder as he goes past. I turn to watch him go, knowing that no one will think anything of it as they're all doing the exact same thing. Very few men can look good in anything, but no matter what Kyle wears, I always want to rip it off him.

When he vanishes out of sight, we all turn back and see that one of the waiters has poured the champagne and cleared away the ice bucket and now empty bottle. There are six glasses filled with bubbly sat there waiting for us. I pick up the one nearest to me and feel my phone vibrate in my pocket. Pulling it out, I see it's a text from Kyle.

Enjoy the champagne. I'll see you, all of you, later. Just so you know, my connecting door is unlocked.

I'm meant to be enjoying a few drinks with the girls before the party, but knowing that Kyle is upstairs in his room, all alone, looking all kinds of sexy... there's no way I'm going to be able to concentrate on any conversation we might have. Then again, if I say I'm going up to my room almost right after Kyle has left us, it might leave us open to gossip. Of course, I could just be over thinking it, and no one would think anything of it, but I'm not going to risk it.

No, I'm going to enjoy my glass of champagne, make idle chit chat for at least thirty minutes, and try my hardest not to think about the man who is going to be rolling around naked with me later on tonight. Then again, the way he looks in a tux, I might just get him to stand there so I can look at him, because that is one sight I will never get tired of.

After another half an hour has passed, the champagne has been drunk and we've only two hours before the party starts. I didn't get a chance to do much with my hair last night due to Kyle's surprise sleepover. I managed to wash it, with Kyle's help—or maybe it was a hindrance; I've not decided yet—but that's about it. I need to do something with it tonight, which means I need to get going if I'm going to be ready on time.

"If you'll all excuse me, girls, I'm going to head up to my room. I shall see you all at the party later. Don't forget to save me a seat."

"Oh, I think the seats are assigned, Ellie. There should be a table plan just inside the room when the doors open," Eliza informs me.

"Really?" Why did I not know about this? "Who did the plan?"

"No idea. I'm assuming Kevin and Kyle, seeing as they organised everything else. See you later, Ellie."

As I walk towards the lifts, I try and figure out whether Kyle would really be stupid enough to sit me at the same table as him, or worse, right next to him. No, Kevin wouldn't let him do that, at least I hope he wouldn't. Getting through tonight is going to be hard enough as it is without being sat in such close proximity to Kyle. Other side of the room: that's the only thing that's going to make it a bit easier for me to enjoy the evening.

After a few minutes, I reach my room and take the key card out of my bag to unlock the door. When the light flashes green, I enter, and see my dress laid out on the bed. Kyle has no idea what the dress is like, even what colour it is. I know his eyes are going to pop out of his head when he sees me.

The white chemise he gave me yesterday is hanging on the front of the wardrobe, and I can't wait to put it on for him later.

Glancing over, I see the door that connects my room to his and know that he is on the other side. It would be so easy to go over, open it, and fall into his arms, but I know if I do that neither of us will make it down to the party, which would well and truly let the cat out of the bag.

Trying to ignore that he is so close, I cross the room and go into the bathroom, closing the door behind me. After stripping out of my clothes, I put on the robe Kyle bought me and look at myself in the mirror. I brought my straightening iron and my curler, mainly because when I packed, I still hadn't decided what to do with my hair tonight.

Deciding to do my makeup first, I go through my usual routine of cleansing then priming my skin, before applying a light layer of foundation. After putting on mascara, I look at the three eye shadow palettes I brought with me, and smile when I apply a glittery colour to match my dress. It's a bold colour, and so unlike me, but when it's finished, I love how the colour makes my eyes look like they're sparkling.

Because I've gone all out on my eyes, I choose a soft pink for my lips, and when I'm finished, I've decided that I'm going to curl my hair. I wear it straight more often than not, and usually in a ponytail for work just to keep it out of my face.

Pulling the clips out of my wash bag, I section my hair and spend the next forty-five minutes making sure every section of hair is curled and fixed into place with a little hairspray.

Now, for the dress.

Walking out of the bathroom, I head over to the bed, when I hear a knock at the door, but it's not the main door, it's the door that connects my room to Kyle's. I knew he wouldn't be able to wait until after the party, then again, it was fifty-fifty who would cave first.

I cross over to the door and place my palm on the wood. I so want to open this door, but I know if I do, several things will happen. We'll wind up naked, my hair and makeup will be ruined, and he will see my dress. While I definitely want to end up naked with Kyle, I want it to be at the end of the night, when he's spent all evening seeing me dressed up in an outfit I never thought I would have the guts to wear.

"Hello Kyle," I say through the door.

"Ellie? Open the door."

"Can't do that," I tell him.

"Why not? Come on, Ellie, I need to see you."

And I need to see him. Is he already in his tux, or is he shirtless with just the trousers on? He could be in his underwear, or naked for all I know, and even though the images I have of him in my head are delicious, I have to stay strong.

"I want to surprise you, Kyle. I want to surprise you with the dress, the hair, the makeup, everything. Let me do that, and I promise I'll let you do anything you want to me later tonight."

"Anything?"

I laugh at his question, knowing that would be what he would pick up on first.

"Yes, anything. Now, go away, I need to get ready."

"Okay, Ellie, I'll let you go. Oh, and Ellie?"

"Yes, Kyle."

"You'll look amazing, whatever you're wearing."

Damn him, he knows just what to say to make me smile. Now I really want to open the door and throw myself at him, but instead, I place my hand on the door, imagining him doing the same on his side, before heading back over to the bed, where my dress is laid out.

I take a moment to just look at it, still not quite believing that I'm actually going to be wearing it tonight. It's a halter neck with thin straps that criss-cross down my back to just above my backside. The low cowl neckline comes down to my belly and has a barely-there mesh insert to maintain my modesty, which can't be seen unless you're up close, which makes it look even more daring from a distance. The satin bodice is fitted to my waist before skimming my hips and falling away into a full-length, a-line skirt with a thigh high split.

Oh, and the best thing about it? It's a bright emerald green colour, which is sure to catch the eye. The dress is designed to grab attention, which I'm sure it will do, from everyone going to the party, but there is only one man I want to grab tonight. I just wish I could do more than just look at him from afar.

After taking a deep breath, I remove the robe and slip on a scrap of material that is meant to pass as underwear and undo the clip at the back of the dress, before stepping into it. The material feels soft against my skin, and as I ease the bodice over my hips and fasten the clasp behind my neck, I feel the butterflies take flight in my belly as I think about the first time Kyle will see me in it.

Walking over to the mirror, I'm a little taken aback by how I look. Not three months ago, I never would have worn a dress like this. I'd have called it too revealing, and not at all me, but now, I've got a newfound confidence. I *can* pull off a dress like this and look good doing it.

After ten more minutes, I'm ready to go. I've put my lipstick, phone and a bit of money in my clutch bag, which is black with green sparkles and matches the shoes I'm wearing, which are black satin with a four-inch glittery green stiletto heel. I've snapped a quick selfie for Becky, after promising I would, and I'm sending it to her, just as a message comes through from Kyle to tell me he's on his way down.

I've already received one from Mel to say she and her partner were going to the bar to meet up with everyone else. So, after giving myself a little pep talk, I leave my room and head down.

30

$\mathcal{A}$s I walk into the bar, I see a crowd of people, each with a drink in their hand, and then hear a squeal as Eliza hurries over to me.

"Oh my God, Ellie, that dress is fabulous."

"Thanks, Eliza, yours looks great too."

She's wearing a deep gold dress that looks great with her skin tone, and as I look at the crowd, I can see all sorts of different colours, from pink to red to purple. So far, not one colour has been duplicated. We couldn't have planned it better if we'd tried.

All the men are in their tuxedos, and I'm beginning to think it's impossible for a man to look anything but gorgeous when wearing one. Either that, or all the women from the office have ridiculously good-looking partners.

"Come on, let's get you a drink before we all head inside. Apparently, Kevin and Kyle are already in there, and I hear they're both looking good, but Kyle in particular is looking fantastically hot tonight. Whoever he's seeing is a lucky girl."

Okay, that gets my attention.

"Kyle is seeing someone?" I ask, trying to ask as nonchalantly as I can.

"That's what the rumour mill is saying. No one knows who the mystery woman is, but she's a damn lucky bitch if she gets to see that man without his clothes on."

I nod at Eliza and smile when a glass of champagne is pushed into my hands. I don't get a chance to think about the rumours as everyone starts the introductions of those partners I've not yet met, and once Jamie arrives to join us, we all head to the function room.

As we near the door, I can see part of the giant easel that holds the seating chart, and I don't know why, but I've a feeling I'm going to be sat by Kyle. Everyone shuffles forward, and as before, I feel him before I see him. As the crowd starts to clear and walk off in the direction of where they'll be sat, I see Kevin first. He's standing by the door, greeting people as they arrive. A handshake for the men and a kiss on the cheek for the women.

Eliza was right, he is looking good. As I near him, I see his brother standing by his side, and Lord above, I think I'm going to combust. I have to take a deep breath to try and steady my heart, but when he sees me and his eyes instantly darken, I know the dress has had the desired effect.

"Ellie, you look lovely this evening," Kevin says as he places a kiss on my cheek. "I hope you have a good night."

"Thank you, Kevin," I say, before taking a step forward until I'm standing in front of Kyle.

Instead of a kiss on my cheek, Kyle takes my hand in his, lifts it to his lips and places a gentle kiss on my knuckles. He never takes his eyes off mine, and I swear the temperature rises several degrees from his look alone. I hope to God no one is near enough to hear my quick breathing or see the effect he is having on me.

"Have a good evening, Miss Fox."

"I'm sure I will, Mr Brendan."

He smirks at my response, and I'm probably the only one close enough to hear the huskiness of his voice. As I move towards the seating chart, I see right away that I was right. I have been sat at the same table as Kyle. I glance back at him to see him chatting with Jamie, but his eyes are still on me, and I have to force myself to move away from him, otherwise everyone is going to know what's going on between us.

As well as me and Kyle, Kevin, his wife and a few others, Jamie and Isobel are also sat at the same table, so at least I'll have someone to talk to, to try and keep me distracted. The only saving grace is that I'm not sat right next to him, and it was probably Kevin that put a stop to that happening.

I weave my way through the dozen or so circular tables that have been set up for the evening, seeing that Eliza and Mel are sat on the table next to mine. All the tables have been decorated in crisp white linen, with sparkling crystals and candles as a centrepiece. I change direction when Eliza calls me over.

"Ellie, did you get a load of Kyle? I mean, holy fuck."

"Well, he's a little hard to miss," I say with a small laugh.

"We're taking bets on whether or not the girl he is supposed to be seeing works with us. What do you think?"

"Oh, I don't think she does," I say, knowing I need to get them off that train of thought, and quickly. "Most are married or in relationships, which leaves three, including me. I highly doubt I'd be able to keep quiet about it if I were sleeping with a guy like Kyle."

"I suppose you have a point," Eliza says, looking defeated. "Still, how cool would it be if it were someone here?" she says as she looks around the room, which is quickly filling up.

Knowing that Eliza seems to be dead set on figuring out who Kyle is seeing, I know that means I need to be more careful about how I act around him, especially tonight. One slip up and I could let the cat out of the bag.

"Ellie, it seems we're sat next to each other."

I smile as Jamie comes to stand next to me and hands me another glass of champagne to replace the one I've not long finished. I tell Mel and Eliza I'll come over and chat later as Jamie and I walk the few feet to our table. A quick glance sees me sat between him and Isobel, who is sat next to Kyle. While I'm glad that there is someone between us, it's still too close. I'm already finding it hard not to look at him every chance I get.

"That has to be another of Chloe's dresses. She really knows what looks good on you."

"Thank you," I reply as Jamie pulls out my seat so I can sit. "It's such a shame she couldn't come tonight," I say as Jamie takes his seat next to me, while two others join us at our table.

"I know, she was really looking forward to it as well. She doesn't get a chance to wear a fancy dress very often. She had one all picked out too. Did you know she used to work at Creativity?"

"No, I didn't. What did she do?"

"She worked reception before I started. She was leaving to open up the shop, and I was her replacement. That's how we met."

I nod as I listen to Jamie. At least now I understand how Chloe knows Kyle and Kevin. I assumed it was through Jamie working there, but knowing she was there before Jamie puts a fresh spin on things, and has me wondering if opening the shop was the real reason she left.

"Did she work at the company long?"

"Just over a year, I think it was. It was only ever a stop gap until she could get the money together to open the shop. Of course, she was never going to stay there long after what happened between her and Kevin. I think the shop was just the reason she tells people."

Kevin? Something went on between her and Kevin? But he's married, with two boys. Surely Kevin didn't cheat on his wife with Chloe. My questions must be written all over my face as Jamie continues.

"It was before Kevin met his wife. They had a fling. Chloe wanted more, Kevin didn't. She doesn't know that I know about it. Chloe tends to let the words tumble out of her mouth when she's had a drink. She told me about it, albeit unwittingly, several years ago. The next morning she'd forgotten all about it. What happened was before we even knew each other so I don't let it bother me."

"And working with Kevin isn't a problem?"

"Not in the slightest. He was single, she was single, and I wasn't in the picture. What Chloe did before I came along doesn't matter to me. She's with me now, and that's all I care about."

I nod at Jamie's words and take a sip of my champagne. At least I don't have to hide anything from him now, which is a relief, as I hate keeping things from my friends.

The room is beginning to fill up quickly, and as more people join our table, I settle in to enjoy the evening.

Two hours later, the food has been eaten and the tables cleared. The lights have been dimmed and the band are getting ready to play their opening set. So far, I think I've dealt with Kyle being so close really well. We've managed to maintain a professional front, and our conversations have been civil and friendly. Although, I'm pretty sure if Isobel wasn't sat between us, his hand would be on my thigh.

Isobel looks stunning in a silver column dress, which I recognise as one of Chloe's as I saw it in the shop when I went to try mine on. She's woven crystals through her red hair, which sparkle in the lights, and has gone for smoky eyes and a bright red lipstick. She looks so different to how she usually looks in the office. Then again, we all do.

As the band begins to play a slow dance classic, I watch as several couples get up to utilise the dancefloor. When Kyle stands, looking at me, for a horrible moment, I think he's going to ask me to dance, but when he turns his attentions to Isobel, I breathe out as she accepts his offered hand and they walk to the dancefloor.

I watch them as he takes her in his arms and moves her effortlessly around the dancefloor. I know I shouldn't be jealous. We need to be discreet tonight. But it's proving to be harder than I thought it would be, especially seeing another woman in his arms.

Accepting a glass of champagne from one of the waiters, I continue chatting to Jamie about the kids he shares with Chloe, when I see Kyle and Isobel coming back to the table just as another song starts. Isobel returns to her seat, but Kyle stops by me, and I know instinctively what's coming.

"Ellie, would do like to dance?"

Like he did with Isobel, he holds out his hand. I know I should refuse him, but that would probably cause more surprise amongst the others here than accepting it would, so I hold out my hand to his, and stand. Kyle escorts me to the edge of the dancefloor and I move into his arms, catching the scent of his aftershave.

I notice that he's careful not to pull me too close, which

I'll admit I'm a little disappointed about, but I'm in his arms, at least for now, and I'm happy about that.

"You know," Kyle begins, "I'm going to have to dance with every woman here, so it doesn't look like I'm singling you out."

"Well that would get tongues wagging," I say with a smile, "considering people are talking about your mystery woman." Kyle raises an eyebrow in question. "Rumours are going round that you're seeing someone, and some people are trying to figure out if it's anyone at work."

"Are they now. Isn't that interesting. I wonder what they'd say if I kissed you right now," he says with a glint in his eye. "Because I've wanted to do more than kiss you since I saw you in that dress. You look stunning, Ellie. Breath-taking."

I can't help but blush at his words and give him a small smile. I'm about to reply, when I feel a tap on my shoulder. Turning, I see it's Jamie.

"Ellie, I'm sorry to interrupt, but I've just had Chloe on the phone. Your friend Becky has been trying to get hold of you. Something's happened to your brother."

I feel Kyle's hold on me tighten slightly as I begin to shake in his arms.

"Eric? What's happened?"

"I don't know the details. I really think you should call your friend."

Not waiting, I glance at Kyle, who just nods, and both men follow me back to the table. Pulling my phone out of my bag, I look at the display to see I have over a dozen missed calls from Becky and one from my parents. If that wasn't enough to alert me to something being wrong, nothing would. I've spoken with my parents just a handful of times since moving here.

Hitting Becky's name, the phone dials her number, and she answers almost immediately.

"Ellie, thank God."

"Becky, what's happened? What's wrong with Eric?"

"Ellie, he's been in an accident." I hear the words and I feel myself begin to sway before hands on my waist steady me. I know it's Kyle, and I let myself lean into him, not caring that people can see us. "You need to come home, Ellie."

"I'll come back tonight. Stay with him, Becky, please."

"They won't let me in the room with him as I'm not family, but I'm not moving from this hospital until you get here."

Becky ends the call and I turn to Kyle, who is removing is jacket and putting it around my shoulders. I didn't realise how cold am I until now.

"Go and get changed. I'll meet you in reception," Kyle orders.

"No, Kyle, I'll be fine."

"No, Ellie, I'm not letting you drive four hours at this time of night when you're clearly in shock." He looks at Kevin, who is now watching us curiously. "Kev, I need to take Ellie back to Bristol. She's just had some bad news."

"Is everything okay?" Kevin asks as he comes around the table to stand by my side.

"Ellie's brother has been in an accident. I need to take her home," Kyle says as he moves closer, practically pulling me to his side.

"Kyle, I don't think that's such a good idea," Kevin almost whispers.

"No, Kev, I'm taking her," Kyle responds.

"Kyle I—"

"I'm not arguing with you about this, brother. I'm taking

Ellie back tonight and I'll be back when I'm sure she's going to be okay." I glance between the two brothers, and it's clear that Kevin doesn't like that his brother is doing this for me, but what Kyle says next shocks everyone within earshot. "You'd do the same thing for the woman you love, and you know it."

I hear several gasps from the people around us, and a long exhale from Kevin. When he reaches out and touches my arm, I look up at him.

"Look after yourself, Ellie," he says with a small smile. "If you need anything, just call."

I nod at Kevin before feeling Kyle take my hand and lead me out of the room, our secret well and truly out.

31

---

alk about rollercoaster emotions. I think I've experienced them all tonight. Excitement at the thought of seeing Ellie in her dress, pure lust when I eventually did see her, and worry when she got the call from her friend. Somewhere along that emotional journey, I realised that I love her.

There was no way in hell my brother was going to stop me from bringing her home tonight, and it took me telling him I loved her to get him to back off. Of course, he wasn't the only one who heard my declaration, so I'm pretty sure Ellie and I are going to be the talk of the office for the foreseeable future, especially if what Ellie said is true and people are already gossiping about who I'm seeing.

It wasn't how I had planned on telling her I love her, and even though she hasn't mentioned it, I know she heard me. Right now, she's sat next to me on the passenger seat, fast asleep. We're about thirty minutes away from Bristol and it's almost one in the morning.

Right now, I'm running on adrenaline and this newfound feeling of protectiveness I have for Ellie. As soon as Jamie came over to us, I saw from his expression that whatever he wanted to say wasn't good. When he said something had happened to her brother, instinct kicked in and I held onto her tightly, wanting her to know I was there.

When she'd been on the phone to her friend, I heard her say Eric had been in an accident, and any colour Ellie had in her had drained from her face, and I grabbed her when she swayed, her free hand splaying on my thigh as she leaned into me.

I knew my brother wouldn't be happy with me taking Ellie back to Bristol. If Ellie didn't work for us, he wouldn't have a problem, and I know he's thinking of the business, but in that moment, my only concern was Ellie and making sure she was okay.

As I led her from the room, I was well aware of the eyes on us. Not everyone would have heard my declaration, so the rumour mill would be doing overtime over the weekend.

I waited for Ellie in reception, wanting to give her some space to breathe if she wanted it. She came down after five minutes wearing jeans and a t-shirt. She'd removed her makeup and put her hair up in a ponytail, and it struck me how young she looked. I could tell she had shed a few tears, and after telling the hotel manager we had to check out early, I told them to allow my brother and Isobel into our rooms to collect our things, and we set off for Bristol.

I glance at the sat nav and see we are less than a mile from the hospital. Becky sent Ellie the details after they spoke, and I recall making a mental note to thank her when I saw her. I'm grateful that Ellie has a friend like Becky, but at the same time, I'm pissed that she had to hear the news from her friend rather than her family. Why the hell hadn't her parents called her?

When I make the turn that leads us into the hospital car

park, I find a space and switch off the engine, turning to Ellie. She's still asleep, my tuxedo jacket over her shoulders. Reaching out, I gently shake her arm until her eyes flutter open and she looks at me.

"Hey, we're here."

She smiles at me and sits up. For a moment, I think she's forgotten what's happened. It's not until she sees where we are that her expression changes, and she goes to jump out of the car. I have to move quickly to catch up with her, and I do so by the entrance to the hospital. I grab her hand, and she pauses a moment before squeezing mine as we walk into the hospital reception.

"Ellie."

We both turn at the sound of Ellie's name, and she releases my hand and flies into the arms of her friend. I watch as the two women hug, and I can see Ellie is crying again. My heart is breaking for her right now, but I know she knows I'm here for her, and when she breaks the hug and comes back to my side, I reclaim her hand with mine.

"How is he, Becky?" I ask, giving Ellie a chance to compose herself.

"Critical but stable. I don't know the extent of his injuries as I'm not family, and your mum and dad are pretty much keeping me out of the loop."

"Where are they?" Ellie asks, her voice strong.

"Last I saw they were in the waiting room while the doctors got Eric settled."

Ellie nods and reaches into her bag, passing her phone to Becky.

"Can you text Arron for me and let him know? His number should be in a message from my brother," she says to her friend, before turning to me. "Will you wait here with Becky? I need to go see them by myself."

"Of course. You know where I am if you need me."

"I know. Thank you." She angles her face and I lean in, placing a gentle kiss on her lips before she releases my hand and moves away. Stopping for a moment, she looks back. "What you said back at the hotel," she says, and I nod, knowing what she's referring to. "I do too."

She smiles at me before she carries on walking, and I glance at Becky, who is also smiling at me. As we sit, I turn to her.

"I'm guessing you've figured out what that was about? Thought so," I respond when she nods. "I need to thank you for letting her know about her brother. If you hadn't, I don't think she would have found out."

"I'm just gutted it ruined your party. She was really looking forward to it."

"What's the deal with her parents? Why weren't they the ones to let her know?"

I watch as Becky sighs and sits back in her seat.

"Ellie has never been close to her parents. Eric is the golden boy. He can do nothing wrong in their eyes, whereas everything Ellie seems to do they have a problem with. Best thing she ever did was move away."

"How did you find out about what happened?"

"Ellie's mum called me. Apparently they tried to call her, and when she didn't answer, they called me and asked if I could try and get hold of her because, and I quote, 'they didn't have the time to keep calling her when their son needed them, and she couldn't be bothered to answer.' Yeah, like Ellie isn't their child too."

I just nod at Becky, who clearly doesn't think much of Ellie's parents, and from the few things I've heard about them, neither do I. I look in the direction that Ellie went, wishing I could be there with her right now, but she knows

I'm here, and I'm not going anywhere.

32

*A*fter asking a nurse where Eric is, I'm now standing outside the waiting room where I know my parents are waiting for news on my brother. Before I go in there, I need to know how my brother is, so I look around, seeing a doctor coming down the corridor.

"Excuse me, doctor, I'm trying to find out information on Eric Fox. I'm his sister."

"Miss Fox, I'm your brother's consultant. He's holding his own at the moment. We took him in for surgery and repaired all the damage caused by the accident. Thankfully, there was no damage to any of the major organs, or we'd be having a different conversation right now. He's still not out of the woods, but he came through the surgery well, so he's got a fighting chance of pulling through. He's in room 141, just down the hall, if you want to go and see him, but try not to make it longer than ten minutes as he needs to rest as much as he can."

"Is he conscious?" I ask.

"He's in and out because of the drugs we had to give him, but you should be able to speak with him briefly."

"Thank you, doctor."

As the doctor leaves, I head down the hall until I come to room 141. Peering through the small glass window, I see my brother lying in bed. There are tubes and wires all around him.

I wish Kyle was with me right now. I know he's only a few feet away in the waiting room, but I want him by my side. I still can't quite believe that he drove four hours to get me here, even declaring to his brother that he loved me in order to get him to agree.

Even though my mind had been on Eric, hearing those words meant everything to me, and the fact that Kyle said them in front of everyone, not worried about what they may think, meant even more.

As soon as I've seen Eric, and I know he will be okay, I'll go back to Kyle, or at the very least, ask a nurse to go and get him. I'm about to open the door when I hear a male voice asking after my brother. I smile as I realise who the man is and walk up to where he is speaking with one of the nurses.

"Arron?" I say, and the guy turns to me. I know it's him as soon as I see his face.

He is just as my brother described him, and even though they've only been seeing each other for a couple of weeks, I know Eric is completely smitten with the tall, dark-haired mechanic.

Eric called me almost three weeks ago to say he had met someone. I assumed it was a girl, but when he said it was the rugged mechanic who was working on his car, I had the biggest smile on my face. After a week, Eric asked me to call Arron, purely so I could verify that Eric was right when he'd said to me that he had the sexiest voice out there.

I'd done what he'd asked, on the pretence of needing my

car fixed, and reported back that, yes, Arron did have a nice voice, but Kyle's was still top of the charts for me.

"Ellie?" he says and gives me a quick hug. "Where is he? Can I see him?"

I assure the nurse that it's okay for Arron to be here, and I'm about to take him down to Eric's room, when my mum comes out of the waiting room. It's the first time I've seen her since I moved to the coast, and I don't know if it's the time away or because she's worried about Eric, but she looks older than her fifty-five years.

Her short dark hair is as neat and tidy as it usually is, and there are a few more lines on her face than I remember. I'd expected to see she'd been crying, but there is nothing to indicate she has been. Her simple black trousers and white blouse are perfect, even at this time of night. She's even got makeup on. You'd think she was going to a job interview, not sitting in a hospital waiting room.

"Eleanor. It's nice of you to come," my mum says, looking at Arron as she's talking to me.

"He's my brother. Of course I came."

"Is this your boyfriend?"

I can almost hear the distain in her voice as she looks between us, just as my dad comes to stand next to her. Like my mum, he is just as put together as he always in. Perfectly pressed trousers and shirt, but he's stopped short of the tie he usually wears every day. His salt and pepper hair is neatly groomed, and his grey eyes are as suspicious as always. Some would consider him to be a handsome man, even at sixty, but to me, especially with the way he's looking at me now, his personality makes him ugly.

Yes, I know that's a horrible thing to say about my own dad, but after years of being told I'll never amount to anything, so much so that you almost start to believe it, it's hard to see him any other way.

"This is Arron, he's a friend of Eric's. He heard what happened and wanted to come and make sure he's going to be okay."

I hate lying, especially when Arron is standing right next to me, but I know Eric won't want our parents to know about their relationship. Not just yet anyway.

"Oh, well, it's nice to meet you, Arron. Eleanor, your friend Rebecca is here somewhere."

"I know, I saw her in reception. She's with Kyle."

"And who's Kyle?" she asks me.

"He's my boyfriend."

I feel a tingle run through me. That's the first time I've called Kyle my boyfriend, but I figure that's officially what we are now. I'm guessing that after Kyle dropped the "L" bomb at the party, we are the only topic of conversation amongst the staff. I've no idea what awaits me, what awaits us, when we go back to Porthcurno, but that's not important now. Eric is what's important.

"You brought your boyfriend to the hospital?" my father asks.

"Yes. When I found out about Eric, no thanks to you, I was with him at a party, so he drove us here so I could get some rest before arriving."

I hadn't wanted to make a scene at the hospital, but there is just something about my parents that pushes my buttons, and I can see by the colour rising in my father's face that I've pushed a button in return.

"Now just a minute, young lady, we tried to call you, but you couldn't be bothered to answer."

"You called me once! Once, Dad! My brother was fighting for his life in surgery and you could only be bothered to try and call me once before palming the job off on Becky. I should have heard the news from you or Mum, but I guess that was too much trouble for you."

I don't realise how loudly I'm speaking until I see Becky and Kyle coming down the corridor. Clearly, they heard my voice, and judging by the fact that Becky is trailing behind Kyle, he is probably the one who was worried about what was going on.

"Is everything okay?" Kyle comes right to my side and wraps an arm around my shoulder. "Is your brother—?"

"No, no. The doctor said Eric has a good chance of pulling through. I was just speaking with my parents. Mum, Dad, this is Kyle."

"Mr. Fox, Mrs. Fox. I'm sorry about your son."

Neither one of my parents acknowledges Kyle as they turn to each other and head back into the waiting room. I feel my temper rising, and Kyle must be able to tell as he pulls me into him and holds me.

We stand there for several minutes, just holding each other as Arron and Becky chat, trying to ignore our moment. I hate my parents right now, but I refuse to cry. My emotions are all over the place, and it would be so easy for me to let go, so when Kyle starts rubbing my back, I take a deep breath and close my eyes. When I pull away a few minutes later, I'm feeling a little calmer.

"Thanks for that," I say to him. "And sorry about my parents."

"Don't be. They're upset about your brother."

"I wish that were true," I say with a small smile. "Oh, Kyle, Becky, this is Arron. He's Eric's boyfriend."

After the introductions are over with, Becky gives me a hug and tells me she is going to head home. She's been there for several hours, just because I couldn't be, so I owe her big time.

"If you and Arron want to go and spend a bit of time with Eric, I can wait here for you."

"You sure? I'll just go in and make sure he's okay, then we can leave," I say to him, remembering that we have nowhere to go.

"Don't worry, I sorted us a hotel while I was in reception. And take as long as you need."

"I swear, sometimes I think you can read my mind."

I give him a kiss before leaving him in the corridor and heading down to see my brother.

33

I watch Ellie and Arron vanish into a room down the hall and turn to the waiting room. I know Ellie won't appreciate what I'm about to do, but I need to speak with her parents. She doesn't know, but I heard her conversation with them and I heard the pain in her voice as she confronted them.

Becky tried to stop me, but there was no way I was going to leave her on her own with them. Like it or not, Ellie and I are a unit now, which means when she needs me, I'm there.

I enter the room to see her parents sat on a bench. They're not talking, and not touching, which I immediately think is strange. If it were Kevin or I in that hospital bed, our mum would be inconsolable, and Dad would be pacing the floor, demanding answers.

It's not until I close the door and move to sit opposite them that they even acknowledge I'm there, and the looks on their faces is anything but pleasant.

"So, how long have you and Eleanor been together?" Mr. Fox asks.

"Not long," I reply, deciding honesty is best with people like these.

"You've not been together long, yet you drop everything to drive her back up here in the early hours of the morning?"

I hear the tone in her father's voice and can tell he either doesn't believe we've only been together a short time, or he thinks I'm after something.

"Yes. She needed me. She was in no state to drive. I don't see anything strange about that. It's what people do when they care for someone." I sit forward so my forearms are resting on my knees, and I look between her parents. "I need to ask you both something." When neither of them indicates that is a problem, I continue. "Why didn't you try harder to reach your daughter to let her know about Eric?"

"Young man, that's none of your business," Mrs. Fox responds.

"Now, you see, that's where you're wrong, Mrs. Fox. By not hearing what happened from you, you hurt Ellie. As you've probably gathered by now, I care about Ellie, so that makes it my business."

"We tried calling her, but she didn't answer. She never answers."

"According to Ellie, you tried calling her once. One time before you gave up. Do want to know how many times Becky tried before she got hold of her? Twenty. And when she couldn't get through on her own phone, she found a way to get a message to her through a friend." When neither of them responds to what I've said, I sit back. "Look at you two. Your son is lying in a bed down the hall, and nothing. There is no emotion from either of you. Don't you care about your children at all?"

"That's none—"

"Yeah I know, that's none of my business." I stand and go

to leave, before turning back to them. "You have a wonderful daughter, and if you just bothered to look at her, really look at her, you'd see what you're missing out on."

They don't say anything as I leave the room, and I see Ellie walking towards me. She smiles as she nears and wraps her arms around my waist as mine go round her back. I feel her relax as she sighs deeply before looking up at me.

"How's he doing?" I ask her.

"Considering what he's been through, he's doing okay. I left Arron in there so they could have a few minutes on their own."

"That's nice of you, and how're you doing?"

"I'm okay, better now I've seen Eric. I'm just so tired. I could sleep for days."

"Well, let's get to the hotel and get some sleep. We can come back and see Eric in the morning."

I smile when she nods and hugs me tighter, and I turn to lead her from the hospital.

"Eleanor."

We both turn back to see her mother standing outside the waiting room, but this looks like a different woman to the one I was talking to only a few minutes ago. It's clear she has been crying, and when she holds out her arms to her daughter, Ellie leaves my side and walks into them. I watch as mother and daughter embrace before pulling apart.

"I'm sorry, Eleanor. We should have tried harder to contact you. It's just, when you didn't answer, we thought you were ignoring us. We figured you would answer the phone straight away to Rebecca, seeing as you two are so close. We didn't realise you were at a party and that it would take so long for her to get hold of you."

"Why would you think I was ignoring you?" Ellie asks.

"Come on, Eleanor, you never answer the phone when we

call you. Since you've been at this new job, how often have we spoken?"

"But you never call—"

"And you never call us either." Both women stop talking and just allow that information sink in, before Mrs. Fox continues, "Eleanor... Ellie, I know we haven't been the best parents, but we do love you. How is your new life? Your job?"

I watch the two women talking, and it seems Mrs. Fox is extending an olive branch to Ellie, but the question is, will she accept it? I see Ellie look back at me, before looking back to her mother.

"The job is going great. I work with a lot of good people, and I've made new friends, and as for my life..." Ellie turns and extends her hand to me, which I take as I move to stand beside her, "...my new life is even better."

"Your young man certainly made an impression on me and your father," she says, before directing her next words to me. "I know you care about my daughter, so I'm trusting you to look after her when we can't. Can you do that?"

"With my life."

Ellie's mum nods, appearing happy with my response. She turns when she hears footsteps behind her, seeing Arron coming towards us.

"Arron, is it?" Mrs. Fox asks him and is given a nod in response. "How long have you and my son been together?"

"Oh, they're just friends, Mum." Ellie jumps in, and receives an eye roll from her mother, making me realise where Ellie gets that particular quirk from.

"Ellie, I might be getting old, but I'm not blind. I've known about Eric for some time now."

"But you never said anything."

"It wasn't my place to. I figured when Eric is ready, he

will tell me himself." Mrs. Fox takes a moment to look at us all. "You two should go and get some sleep. You've been up for hours; you must be tired. Ellie, your old room is free if you want to use it. Your father and I are staying here for the night. The nurses are setting up a couple of cots for us."

"Kyle has booked us a hotel, but thank you, Mum."

Mrs. Fox looks at us all one more time, before smiling and returning to her husband in the waiting room. Arron thanks Ellie for letting him be there and then goes, saying he will be back tomorrow, leaving Ellie and I alone, which is when Ellie turns and kisses me.

"What was that for?" I ask as I hold her close.

"I don't know what you said to my parents but thank you."

"I didn't say too much. Just pointed out how great their daughter is, and what they're missing out on. Now, your mum's right. We need to get some sleep."

Ellie smiles and nods as we turn to leave the hospital. After only ten minutes, I am pushing the key card into the lock to open the door to our hotel room. It's not until she's in my arms under the covers that she says something.

"I know this isn't the night we had planned, and I'm sorry for that."

"You have nothing to apologise for. Tonight is perfect because I'm with you. That's all that matters."

"They're all going to be talking about us at work, you know. I bet Kevin's pissed."

"Oh, he'll get over it. He knows how I feel, so he'll make it work somehow."

"After what you said, I think everyone knows how you feel," she says as she shifts position so she can look up at me. "Did you mean what you said?"

I hear the uncertainty in her voice, and I tighten my hold on her as I look down and smile.

"One hundred percent. It wasn't how I'd planned on telling you, and it wasn't until tonight, when I first set eyes on you all dressed up, that I realised that's how I feel, but it is, and I do."

"Say it again?" she asks.

"I love you, Ellie."

Her eyes are tired, but they still sparkle when I say the words, and her smile lights up her face. I want nothing more than to take her in my arms and make love to her right now, but we're both too tired for that. Instead I just listen to her murmur she loves me too before she drifts off to sleep.

34

It's been two weeks since Eric's accident, and the doctors have said he can come home today. He's been improving every day, and I've split my time between the hospital and my parents' house.

Kyle had to return to Porthcurno the Monday after the accident. I've missed him like crazy, and I know he didn't want to leave me, but I insisted he go back. At the end of the day, he has a business to run, and now that me and my parents have sorted a few things out, it's easier for me to be around them.

He's called me several times a day to check in and has even spoken with Eric a few times too. I can't wait for them to meet each other. Both men have overprotective streaks in them, so it's going to be amusing to see how they get along.

Kyle has told me that so far, no one at work has said anything about what happened at the party. A few have asked how I am, and when I'll be coming back, but nothing has been said about us being together. Of course, that could just be because he's the boss, and it's no one else's business, but I've a feeling that when I start back on Monday, the girls, especially Mel and Eliza, will have a few questions for me.

Seeing as Kyle drove me back to Bristol, my car is still down in Porthcurno, so Kyle is driving back up in the morning to pick me up. He's agreed to have dinner at my parents' house before we drive home. My mum is going all out with a full Sunday roast with all the trimmings. It's a good job Kyle has a good appetite, because he's going to need it.

Right now, I'm at the hospital helping Eric get his things together and waiting for the nurse to bring his medication. Arron is at Eric's place, making sure everything is set up for when he gets home, while also moving in a few things of his own. Our parents wanted Eric to go back to theirs while he recovered, but he insisted on going back to his own place. The only way Mum would allow it was if someone was there to look after him, and Arron didn't hesitate in accepting the responsibility.

I must admit, my parents have surprised me with how well they have accepted Arron into Eric's life. Both Eric and I thought they would have a major issue with it, especially Dad, but they've both been great.

While it's sad that it's taken what happened to Eric to bring us together as a family, I think we're finally in a place where we're all happy and content. Now, all I need to do is get through today so I can see Kyle in the morning.

While we've spoken every day and our text sessions have been... stimulating, it's not the same as having the physical man by my side. I can't wait to just hug him and have his arms wrapped around me again. Two weeks is a long time when you're in love, something he tells me every time we speak.

"Here you go, Mr. Fox," the nurse says as she brings in a bag containing Eric's medication. "You'll need to come in next week so we can check how you're doing and see if we need to repeat any of the prescriptions. Now, do you have transport to get home?"

"Yes, my car is outside. My sister is going to drive," Eric tells her.

"Good, now, you look after yourself and take it easy. I don't want to hear any reports of you popping those stitches because you've been out dancing."

Eric laughs at the nurse's comment as she leaves the room. Even though Eric likes guys, he is still a terrible flirt when it comes to women. He tried to impress this particular nurse by bragging about his dancing skills, and while I'll admit my brother can hold his own on the dance floor, he's no Baryshnikov.

"You ready to go?" I ask him as I put the last of his things in a bag.

"You bet. Get me out of this place and back home please, sis."

I put the bag on the end of the bed and move over to Eric, helping him stand and then moving him into the wheelchair one of the orderlies brought in earlier. After putting the bag over my shoulder, I wheel him out of the room and down the hallway. Eric waves at the nurses as he passes and shakes the hand of the doctor that performed the surgery on him.

After only a few minutes, we're outside by the car and I've helped Eric into the passenger seat. Once he's inside, I return the wheelchair and head back to the car, and we're soon on our way back to Eric's.

～

"So, how's Eric doing?"

"He's okay. Majorly happy to be back home."

"Yeah I bet, especially with Arron there playing nurse."

We both laugh at Becky's comment as she pours us another glass of wine. Becky and I made the impromptu decision to come out for a drink before I head back to Porthcurno. She's been a great friend these last two weeks. With Kyle not being here, Becky has been the one I've turned to when I've needed to cry, scream, or just vent. I don't know what I would have done without her.

"What time will Kyle be arriving tomorrow?"

"I'm not sure. He said he will text me when he's leaving, and when he's an hour out."

Just talking about Kyle makes me smile, even though it causes Becky to roll her eyes. I know she's happy for me. If she wasn't, she wouldn't constantly ask about how he's doing, or how we're doing together. I know she's only after the juicy details; details I refuse to give her.

"You know, I still can't quite believe that your one-night stand is now your boyfriend, especially given the circumstances."

"I know. I guess it was just meant to be."

Becky gives me a gagging impression, and I can't help but laugh. Yeah, I know saying it was cliché and a little sappy, but that's the only way I can think of to describe it. I mean, what were the odds that the man I had a fling with in Bristol would turn out to be my boss at a company four hours away in Porthcurno?

"How've things been with you anyway, Becky? We've not had much time to talk about you these last two weeks. Tell me what's been happening?"

"Well, I quit my job, and have three months to find a new place to live."

"Becky, what the fuck? Why didn't you tell me about this?"

"You've got enough going on, and it's no biggie. You know I've always hated working at that place, so it was inevitable really. As for where I'm staying, my landlord wants to reclaim the property so he can do it up and sell it on. I've more than enough time to find somewhere else, so I'm not stressing about it, and neither should you."

I shake my head at Becky and take a sip of my wine. I can't believe she had all of this going on, and she didn't mention it to me. She knows I'll be there for her in any way I can be, but as usual, she's thinking of others instead of herself. It's one of the reasons I love her.

"Anyway," Becky says with a devious smile on her face. "When Mr. Hot Stuff arrives and whisks you off your feet to take you home tomorrow, what's the plan for the rest of the day?"

"Oh, I don't know. I'll unpack, then maybe do some washing. Oh, and I'll need to go and get some shopping in."

I laugh when Becky slaps my arm.

"Talk about ask a stupid question, Becky. What the hell do you think I'm going to do? I've not seen Kyle in two weeks. I don't plan on leaving the bedroom, or wearing clothes, until I have to be up for work on Monday."

"Ah yes, back to work. How do you feel about that?"

"Truthfully, I'm not sure. I mean, I want to go back, as I'm strangely missing being there, but I don't relish being the talk of the office, and I know people will be talking and whispering." I take another sip of wine before I continue, "I don't regret being with Kyle, not for one second. I always knew there was a chance being with him could affect my job, and I thought I prepared for it. I guess I'll just have to wait and see what happens on Monday."

While I can't wait to see Kyle again and to get back to work, like I've just said to Becky, the thought of being the source of gossip amongst the people I work with doesn't sit well. Kyle and I knew that eventually, our relationship would have to come out, but we wanted to do it on our own terms.

The way it happened had been due to outside events. People will have been gossiping and spreading rumours for the entire two weeks I've been away, and while Kyle says no one has said anything directly to him, he knows people are talking.

There's nothing I can do to stop people making assumptions or saying things about us. All I can do is wait until Monday and address any questions anyone might have then.

I've requested a meeting with Kevin first thing, as more than anything, I want to know his position on things. He is the one affected most by my relationship with his brother. He's known about us from pretty much the beginning, so I need to know he is okay with what's happening between us.

Until then, I've no idea what will happen with my job, or even if I'll have a job after Monday. Initially, losing it was the main reason I was resisting being with Kyle, but now, one thing I do know is I will never consider being with Kyle a mistake, even if down the line, it does cost me my career.

35

"For heaven's sake, Eleanor, will you sit down. He'll be here soon."

I see the amusement on my mum's face as I walk past the window for the umpteenth time. Kyle text me half an hour ago to say he was a mile away, yet he still isn't here. To say I'm eager to see him again wouldn't be the right word. I'd go as far to say I'm desperate to see him; to be in his arms again; to feel his skin against mine.

It's been almost two weeks since he returned to Porthcurno, and even though we've talked and texted every day, it's just not the same, and I can't wait until he gets here so I can begin to show him how much I've missed him.

"She's antsy because she hasn't had any for two weeks," my brother pipes up from his spot on the sofa, causing him to receive a glare from our mother.

I'm about to say something in response to Eric, when I hear a car pull up outside. Looking out the window, I recognise Kyle's BMW and race to the door, flinging it open and racing down the drive. I barely give Kyle a chance to get out of the car before I throw myself into his arms.

Within seconds my lips are on his and my arms are locked around his neck. If we weren't in a public place, I'd be climbing his body and wrapping my legs around his waist. As it is, all I can do is hold him and kiss him and hope that is enough to convey how hard not being with him has been for me.

He's holding me just as tightly as I am him, and when we eventually part, I look up to see him smiling down at me.

"Hi."

"Hi," I respond with a small laugh.

"I've miss you so much," he says as he tightens his hold on me. "I can't wait to get you back home." When I look at him, then the car, then back at the house, Kyle laughs. "No, we can't skip dinner."

When I look up and pout, he bursts out laughing and covers my mouth with his in a heart stopping kiss that, when it ends, leaves my head spinning.

"Come on, let's go inside before they send out a search party."

"You sure we can't just get in the car and go home?"

"No, now move that cute ass into the house."

When I turn, he playfully slaps my backside and follows me up the driveway, and we're soon inside. All I can think about is eating dinner and driving home as soon as we can, so I'm relieved when I see my mum has started bringing food out of the kitchen.

"Kyle, thank goodness you're here," my mum says as she places a dish containing peas and carrots on the table. "Eleanor has been pacing in front of that window for the last hour."

"Has she now?" Kyle says as he grins at me.

"Well, you said you were a mile away. What took you so long to get here?"

"I had to make a stop on the way," Kyle says, before turning to Eric, who is sat on the sofa next to Arron. "Eric, good to finally meet you. How're you feeling?"

I watch as my brother eases himself to his feet and walks over to Kyle. As the two most important men in my life shake hands, I'm unable to stop the smile from spreading across my face. It was only two weeks ago that I thought I would lose Eric because of a drunk driver, but he pulled through and is now standing in front of me chatting with my boyfriend.

"Dinner is ready, everyone."

We all turn at the sound of my dad's voice to see the table covered in dishes full of food. Mum has really gone all out, which isn't really surprising. I can't remember the last time both Eric and I were here for Sunday lunch, not to mention here with our partners.

I take Kyle's hand and lead him over to the table, and we take our seats opposite Eric and Arron, with my parents at either end. After my dad pours us each a glass of wine, we all tuck in to one of the best Sunday dinners I've ever had.

$\approx$

After dinner, Kyle and I excused ourselves as soon as we could without seeming rude and started back for Porthcurno. The usual four-hour drive had taken Kyle closer to three, and within seconds of being back home, I was in his arms, letting his hands, tongue and cock do whatever they wanted to me.

We'd done things I've only ever read about in romance novels, and now, three toe curling orgasms later, we're lying in bed, legs tangled, hearts pounding and breathing as fast as the roadrunner evading the coyote.

"That was... wow," I say in between breaths, turning my head to look at him.

"You can say that again," he replies, equally as out of breath as I am.

"I would, but I don't think I can."

We both laugh for a few moments, before falling silent, staying that way for several minutes before I start thinking about something that I've been trying to ignore all day.

Tomorrow.

I've known this day was coming. I've been away for two weeks, and Kevin was gracious enough to let me take it as compassionate leave. How much of that was Kyle's doing, I don't know, but I appreciate it, nonetheless.

Kyle has told me nothing has been said to him about us being together, but they wouldn't say anything to him, would they? He's the boss, after all. If anything, it's me that's going to have to answer all the questions from people.

I know it'll go one of two ways; either people will come up to me and want all the details, or no one will, and they'll just stare at me and whisper behind my back. Even though I've no idea what I'm going to say to people, I'm hoping it's the former. Having people talking about me is a big part of why I was so hesitant to trying to make a go of it with Kyle. If people want to know something, I would rather they just come up to me and ask.

"It will be alright, you know," Kyle says as he runs his fingers up and down my arm. I turn to look up at him.

"How do you always know what I'm thinking?"

"I don't, I just know you. You're worried about what people are going to say or do tomorrow. Well, don't be. Let them think what they like. The only people that matter are you and me. Kevin, to some degree, too. He might have been a bit off with me when he found out, but he's come to terms with it now. He knows how I feel about you, and he knows not to try and stop me from seeing you. Talking of Kevin, do you want me to be with you when you meet with him in the morning?"

"No. Thank you for the offer, but I need to do it on my own. I owe your brother that much."

Kyle nods, leaning down to kiss me on the nose before stretching his arms over his head as his stomach growls, causing me to laugh.

"You can't possibly be hungry after what we had for lunch?"

"You would think that, wouldn't you? But I am."

I shake my head, unable to believe that there is any room left in his stomach for any more food. When I said my mum had gone all out with dinner today, I wasn't kidding. It seemed like she cooked every vegetable you could imagine. She cooked four different types of potato, and three different meats, oh, and not forgetting the condiments to go with each meat. It was a veritable feast, and the six of us practically polished off all of it.

Yet, even after all that, Kyle is hungry. He grabs his phone, and after a brief discussion, orders us an extra-large pepperoni pizza with extra onions and mushrooms. We both, reluctantly, get out of bed, Kyle pulling on his jeans while I grab a t-shirt and shorts. After making us both a cup of coffee, we move to the sofa and wait for our food to arrive.

"I've no idea how you keep those abs with the amount you eat."

"Why do you think Kevin is working on getting a gym put in the basement? We both spend a small fortune at the gym, but if we stop, we both pile the weight on so easily."

"Well, it clearly works for you," I say as I smile at him, then let my eyes roam across his chest, and then his abs.

"Are you eyeing me up, woman?" Kyle asks with a tone I

recognise, and I begin to wish I went to the gym as often as he does.

I go to jump up from the sofa, but he's too quick and has me pulled back down and underneath him in five seconds flat. His hands are working their way under my t-shirt as his lips work their magic on my neck. I'm like putty in his hands, and he knows it. I doubt I'll ever be able to resist him when he has me pinned down like this.

There's something about having his weight on top of me like this, with his hands on my body as his lips do wondrous things to my insides. When he hits a sensitive spot on my throat, I'm two seconds from stripping us both naked, when there's a knock at the door.

I groan as Kyle levers himself up and off me as I move to a sitting position. Kyle accepts the pizza from the delivery driver, pays, and after retrieving something from his bag, returns to the sofa, positioning the pizza on the coffee table and handing me a small black velvet pouch.

"What's this?"

"Open it and see. I hope you like it."

I look at him quizzically as I untie the strings that keep the pouch closed and open it. Holding out my hand, I empty the contents into my palm, gasping at what I see in front of me.

Holding up the silver chain, I look at the pendant. There are several strands of varying length, each with a teardrop of different gemstones. The necklace is gorgeous and is nothing like I've ever owned before.

"Kyle, it's beautiful," I say, tears filling my eyes.

"I'm glad you like it. I got it earlier when I was on my way up to get you. I was almost at your mum's when I got your text. I pulled over to respond, and after I did, I saw I was parked next to a little jewellers, and I saw this in the window. I thought of you straight away."

"I love it, thank you."

Leaning over the pizza box, I give him soft kiss before sitting back down, looking at the necklace again before I carefully place it back in the pouch.

After several minutes and a few slices of pizza later, Kyle speaks.

"I can stay tonight if you like. Maybe we could drive into work together in the morning? I know we've not done it before, to be discreet, but we've no need to be now. What do you think?"

What do I think? I'd love nothing more than to be able to tell the world that I'm with Kyle. That he's my man and I'm his girl. But it doesn't seem right to do that.

"I'm not sure, Kyle. Yes, people know about us, but I don't want to flaunt it, if you know what I mean. Let's just give it a few days, see how my meeting with Kevin goes, how everyone reacts when I'm back, and take it from there." He nods as he stuffs another slice of pizza into his mouth, and I smile. "You can still stay the night though, if you want."

After he's finished devouring the slice in his hands, he wipes his mouth, then leans over to me.

"Oh, you can count on that."

And after those few words, his lips cover mine, and the rest of the pizza is forgotten.

ou can do this, Ellie. These people are your friends.

I give myself a little pep talk as I cross the car park and head towards the main doors. Kyle is still at my place, having agreed to hold back on coming into the office until after my meeting with Kevin. I know he's already here, as his car is parked in his space, as is Isobel's.

I'd be lying if I said I wasn't nervous. I've no idea how this conversation with Kevin is going to go, or even if I still have a job, but there's only one way I'm going to find out.

Pushing through the doors, I see Jamie stand as I walk in. He waves me over, then comes around the reception desk to give me a hug, something that takes me by surprise.

"Ellie, how are you? How's your brother?"

I return Jamie's hug and smile at him when he releases me and steps back.

"I'm fine, and Eric is fine too. He came out of the hospital on Saturday. The doctors are happy with his progress. He just needs to rest as much as he can now."

"That's great news. Chloe sends her love and told me to

tell you she's found something that's perfect for you. Her treat, as a little pick me up."

"Oh, that's sweet, Jamie. Can you pass on my thanks and tell her I'll try and get down to see her at the weekend?"

"Actually, would you mind if I gave you her number? I know she's been worried about you, and even if I tell her you're okay, she won't believe me until she hears it from you."

I smile at his words and hand him my phone from my bag. He quickly enters Chloe's number then passes it back to me. He stays where he is, looking like he wants to ask something but doesn't know how to, and I've a feeling I know what it is. I'm about to say something to him, when he just blurts it out.

"I think you and Kyle are great for each other. There, I said it."

Out of everything, that wasn't what I was expecting him to say.

"Thank you, Jamie. That means a lot," I say, breathing a sigh of relief that at least one of my friends here doesn't think the worst of me.

"Just so you know, since you've not been here, he hasn't been the fun-loving, easy-going Kyle we're all used to. He's been doing his work, no one can fault him there, but he's been really worried about you, Ellie."

I smile, and I'm about to respond when I hear squeals, and before I can turn around, I'm engulfed in hugs as arms wrap around me from behind.

"Oh my God, Ellie, you're back. How are you? Is your brother okay?"

I turn, seeing Eliza, Mel and Beth all staring at me, firing questions.

"Hi girls, we're both fine, thank you. Eric is home now and recovering well."

"That's great news," Eliza says as she checks her watch. "We'd better head up, but we should all have lunch later," she says before giving me another hug, whispering in my ear. "You've been holding out on us, lady, and we want details."

She pulls away, a wicked grin on her face as they head off towards the lift. Eliza has checked in on me several times while I was in Bristol and hasn't once mentioned Kyle. Clearly, now that I'm back, all bets are off, and she wants to know what's been going on.

After the reactions of Jamie and the girls, I'm beginning to wonder what I've been worrying about.

"I should be heading up too," I tell Jamie. "I've got a meeting with Kevin in ten minutes."

"Of course, I'll catch you later, Ellie."

Jamie returns to his position behind the reception desk and I head in the direction of the lifts. Less than two minutes later, I'm walking down the office towards my desk. I get waves from people who are already working, and hear several people call out, "Welcome back, Ellie." This place has become like a second home to me, and if this meeting with Kevin doesn't go well, I'm going to hate having to leave.

When I get to my desk, I see Isobel. She is in her office, putting things from her desk into a cardboard box. She has files and boxes stacked onto a trolley, and the name plate that was on her door is now gone. After putting my bag on my desk, I start to walk to her office to find out what's happening, turning my head when I hear someone call my name.

"Ellie, it's good to see you back. If you're okay, we can start our meeting now?"

"Um, yeah, sure."

Looking towards Isobel's office, I see her looking at me,

her expression unreadable. Turning back to Kevin, he holds his office door open as I step inside. When he closes the door, he moves back to his desk and sits, offering me the seat opposite him. I watch as he pours two glasses of water and hands one to me before smiling.

"How are you, Ellie? It's been a rough couple of weeks for you."

"It has, but I'm okay. I've had people that have helped me through it. You included. Before we start, Kevin, I just want to thank you for allowing me the time off. I know I've not been here long, and you didn't have to let me take as much time as I did, so I just want you to know that I appreciate it."

Kevin nods as he takes a sip of his water, just looking at me. I've never really considered him to be a formidable man, but right now, he's scaring the crap out of me, mainly because I've just seen Isobel packing up her office and he's looking at me as if he's trying to figure out what to say next.

"You've certainly done a number on my brother, Ellie. I don't think I've ever seen him like this."

"So, is that a good or a bad thing?" I say, unsure what else to say in response.

"Oh, it's definitely a good thing," he says as he leans forward. "I'll admit, when Kyle told me about you two, I wasn't happy. Kyle has a history of letting the women in his life get in the way of his work, but with you, he's different. If anything, his work has improved. As for your work, I've not been able to fault any of it since you started here. Which is why making this decision has been so hard for Kyle and me to make, but at the same time, we think it's the right one, and the best one for the company."

I feel my stomach begin to churn as my heart begins to race. This is it. My days at Creativity in Design are coming to an end after only a few weeks, and by the sounds of it, Kyle knew all about it, and said nothing.

"Look, Kevin. I know me seeing Kyle is against company policy, but if you would just—" I begin, but he stops me by holding up his hand.

"I'm not firing you, Ellie," he says, causing me to exhale quickly. "Do you really think I'd let someone with your potential go that easily? I said from the moment Kyle told me about you two that I wasn't going to lose you, and yes, you two seeing each other is against company policy, which is why we found a way around it. Isobel has already been informed of our decision, and now it's my job to tell you too."

"Isobel? What does she have to do with this? I'm so confused right now."

Kevin laughs before standing and moving around his desk to sit in the chair next to me.

"Well, seeing as you are her assistant, and she has told me several times she would be lost without you, I figured if I transfer one, I transfer both of you."

"Sorry, what? Transfer?"

"Before you had to take the time off to be with your brother, you probably noticed Kyle and I had a lot of closed-door meetings." When I nod, he continues, "Well, that was us putting our heads together to try and figure out a way for you two to stay together, without breaking company policy. You've probably noticed this, but my brother can be a stubborn bastard when he wants to be, and there was no way he was giving you up. So, we needed to find a way for me to keep you at the company, and for Kyle to keep you in his life. The result was something we had been considering for a couple of years but never got round to doing. Your relationship with Kyle gave us the push we needed to get it done, and I have to say, we're pretty pleased with the outcome."

"Okay," I say, taking a mouthful of water to try and calm my nerves. "So, what's the outcome?"

Kevin sits back and grins widely at me, picking up a folder from his desk and handing it to me. When I open it, I see photographs and drawings of a beautiful office space. The first few photos are of what looks like a waiting area, with half a dozen comfy chairs, a small table with a water fountain, and tea/coffee machines. The walls are covered in designs, which I recognise as being jobs Isobel and I have worked on.

When I flip the page, I see more photos, this time of two offices separated by a glass wall. Both offices are beautifully decorated with large desks, every piece of technology anyone could need, and a large bookcase filled with books and folders. When I look up from the folder, my expression clearly shows my confusion.

"Ellie, Kyle and I have opened a second office in Porthcurno town. It's going to be managed by Isobel, with you as her assistant/trainee. If people need any design work, they will be referred to the new office to make first contact. It will be your job to meet with potential clients and find out what their requirements are. You will then go through those requirements with Isobel, and then you'll both decide who to assign the project to, having chosen the most appropriate designer for the client's needs."

"So that's why Isobel is packing up?"

"Yes, we open the new office next week, so I need you and Isobel to get set up as soon as possible. It's your space to do with as you wish. This week you can both get it how you like it, ready for the opening on Monday."

I sit back, just looking between Kevin and the folder, realising that while this is a fantastic opportunity, I can't shake the feeling that people will think what I've been worried about this entire time: that the only reason I am getting this move is because of my relationship with Kyle.

"Kyle told me what you were worried about," he says as he leans forward. "About people thinking you'd be given preferential treatment?" I nod, hating that I'm close to tears right now. "Ellie, it's Isobel that got the promotion, and she got it because she is the best designer we have, and she deserves it. You're moving with her as you're her assistant."

"That's just semantics, Kevin, and you know it."

"No, it's not semantics, it's fact. As I said before, we've been considering opening this second office for a while now, and Isobel was always in the running for the job. We've mentioned it to her before and have evidence to back that up. Yes, it was your relationship with Kyle that forced us to make it a reality, but it was always going to be Isobel running the show there, with or without you. So, will you accept the job, Ellie?"

I look at him for several moments, considering everything that he said to me in the last ten minutes, and I know there is only one decision I can make.

"Count me in."

I watch as Kevin breathes out before standing. I follow his lead and hand him back the folder, stopping short of giving him a hug. He tells me to start packing up my desk, as Isobel has a head start on me, before going back to sit behind his desk. As I open the door to head out, I turn back to him.

"Kevin, I take it this means the gym isn't happening?"

I grin at him as he shakes his head and pouts, actually pouts, at me, causing me to laugh as I leave and head back to my desk.

EPILOGUE

"*T*hank you, Miss Mills, we'll be in touch."

I say goodbye to our last client of the day and flip the lock on the door. Isobel is standing in the doorway to her office, and when I look at her, she just rolls her eyes.

"How many is that now?"

"Eight. Eight times she has changed her mind about the design. I wouldn't mind, but the space she has really isn't that big. There are only so many things she can fit in there, but to hear her speak, you'd think she could get a whole showroom in there."

We both laugh as Isobel returns to her office. I can see she has already started to pack up for the weekend, and I know she is going away with her new husband. They've been married for almost two months now. I've never known a wedding be planned and executed so quickly.

From the moment Isobel announced she and Lucas were engaged, they had the whole thing planned within three weeks and were married another three weeks later. Of course, that sparked the inevitable 'she must be pregnant' rumours, which were untrue, but the wedding will always be memorable for me, as it was the first 'event' Kyle and I attended as a couple.

I must admit, thinking back, I feel more than a little stupid for thinking some of the things I did back when Kyle and I were first starting out. Everyone has been great. No one has thought any of the things I'd feared, and all the girls want to know is what Kyle is like outside of work. I give them enough to keep them happy but keep the really private stuff between the two of us.

It's been just over six months since Isobel and I moved into the new office, and I have to say, the vision Kevin and Kyle had for this place was brilliant. I remember the sounds Isobel and I made when we walked into the office for the first time. There were lots of 'oohs' and 'aaahs' as we looked around. The photos Kevin had shown to me didn't do the place justice.

Isobel and I have made the place our own, and for the most part, the brothers leave us alone to do as we see fit. We have a weekly teleconference with them, and a more formal face-to-face meeting once a month. Kevin was right about Isobel being perfect for the job. She has thrived in her new role, and it has given me more time to learn the skills I need to become a full-fledged designer.

"What do you and Kyle have planned for the weekend?" Isobel asks as I lean against her doorframe.

"Nothing much, just a lazy one, I think. Becky is having her boyfriend come over, so I shall be staying at Kyle's to give them some privacy."

Oh yeah, Becky lives with me now. I knew as soon as she told me if I ever needed a roommate, she would be there, that it would happen eventually. Which it did three months ago. She'd had trouble finding work back in Bristol and was determined not to just accept a job for the hell of it. She hated her last place and wanted to work somewhere she could at least enjoy and be happy at, and that just happened to be around the time Jamie and Chloe announced they were expecting baby number three.

Like with her other pregnancies, Chloe suffered from severe morning sickness, resulting in her being unable to work. As it turned out, Jamie mentioned to me that they were looking for someone to look after the place long-term, which is when I thought of Becky. As she had nothing keeping her in Bristol, and Chloe and Jamie already knew her, it was the perfect fit, so Becky upped sticks and moved down to Porthcurno, and into my spare room.

The boyfriend I mentioned is someone we met, or at least saw from afar, the first time Becky came down to visit. She paid another visit about a month after we opened the new office, and we spent the day on the beach, where she set her sights on the blond-haired, golden skinned surfer, who goes by the name Sean. She approached him, they clicked, and they started a casual thing, which became more serious when Becky moved down to the area.

So much has happened in the last six months, and all of it has been for the better. Kyle and I are going from strength to strength. We're past the stage where we text each other all the time, but every time he sends me a message, I still smile when I see his name on the screen.

"Are you and Lucas all packed?"

"We are. I've been packed all week, but Lucas left his to the last minute, as usual. He should be here any minute."

"So should Kyle. He's taking me to the diner up the street before we head to his. I've got a craving for one of their burgers," I say, causing Isobel to laugh.

"I'd be careful using that word, Ellie. People might talk."

It takes me a moment to figure out what she's referring to, and when I realise, I laugh too.

"Good God no. I'm too young for that."

"That might be, but people will still talk," she says before looking at me with a serious expression. "You and Kyle will make great parents one day."

I feel the blush hit my cheeks, and I'm saved from responding when there is a knock at the door. Turning, I see the figures of two men standing outside, knowing it's Lucas and Kyle. Walking over, I open the door and let them in. Lucas kisses my cheek before walking towards Isobel, and Kyle seals his lips over mine in a kiss that never fails to get my blood pumping.

"You ready to go, Iz?" Lucas asks his wife as he kisses her in much the same way Kyle just kissed me.

"Sure am," she says after catching her breath and securing her bag on her shoulder. "Ellie, are you okay to lock up?"

"Of course, you two have a great weekend, and I'll see you on Tuesday."

After Isobel and Lucas leave, I close and lock the door, flipping the privacy screen to active. When I turn, I see Kyle is watching at me, a familiar glint in his eye, one that I choose to ignore. For now, anyway.

"How did your meetings go today?" I ask.

"Oh, boring as ever," he says as he takes a step closer. "How about your day?"

"Quite interesting actually. Two new clients want new extensions kitted out, one as a dining room, and the other as a 'man cave'," I say, using air quotes. "Oh, and Miss Mills came in again, changing her mind. Yet again. But I think we finally got to what she wants."

"Which is?" Kyle asks.

"Everything she can't afford. But I'll work something out."

"I've no doubt you will."

Despite trying my hardest, I can no longer ignore the glint that Kyle has in his eyes right now. He's closing in on my position, and I know exactly what is running through his mind right now. Me, and him, naked.

When he has me where he wants me, with my back to the wall and him at my front, he kisses me gently, before glancing over his shoulder, towards my office.

"Six months, and we've still not christened that desk."

My eyes widen as I realise what he is suggesting, and I'm about to ask if he's joking when he turns back to me and I see the look on his face. It's enough to tell me he is deadly serious, and when he takes my hand and leads me across the room, it only solidifies what I realised all those months ago.

One night with Kyle was never going to be enough.

Printed in Great Britain
by Amazon